I0745175

SIREN

COVEN: BOOK 2

DAVID NETH

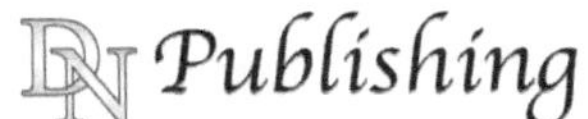

Siren

Coven, Book 2

Copyright © 2021 by David Neth

Batavia, NY

www.DavidNethBooks.com

ISBN: 978-1-945336-11-9
First Edition

Subscribe to the author's newsletter for updates and exclusive content:
DavidNethBooks.com/Newsletter

Follow the author at:
www.facebook.com/DavidNethBooks

Also by David Neth

<u>Coven</u>
Harpy
Siren
Valkyrie
Shapeshifter
Sorcerer
Enchantress
Oracle

<u>Under the Moon</u>
The Full Moon
The Harvest Moon
The Blood Moon
The Crescent Moon
The Blue Moon

The Art of Magic

<u>Fuse</u>
Origin
Omertá
Oblivion

<u>Heat</u>
Black Magnet
Dust Storm
The Gatekeeper

<u>Standalone</u>
All I Ever Wanted

CHAPTER 1

- JULY 1988 -

The truck rocked back and forth as Justin pulled onto the rough gravel parking lot of the Presque Isle Marina. Beside him, his girlfriend Nancy clung to the handle above the door as they maneuvered over the potholes before coming to a resting spot where Justin put the truck in park.

"All right, here we go," he said. "You ready?"

She smiled at him. "I'm going to put on some sun lotion. You should too."

"I will," he promised. "But first I need to run to the locker room and change into my trunks."

"You didn't put them on before you left the house?" she asked, still with a smile.

"Sorry," he said. "Was in too much of a rush to see you." *And*

SIREN

Sandy wouldn't have bought my story that I was going in to work today if I left dressed for a day at the beach.

Justin crossed the parking lot with his backpack slung over his shoulder and went to the locker room. Inside, he began to undress but stopped when he noticed his wedding ring still resting on his finger.

His heart began racing and he quickly replayed every moment he and Nancy had since he picked her up. She hadn't given any indication that she noticed the ring. And it was his left hand, and she was sitting to his right.

With some force and a good measure of twisting and turning, he pulled the ring off and slipped it in the side pocket of his backpack, zipping it back up for safe keeping. It would need to go back on before he went home to Sandy.

Back outside, Justin tossed his bag in the back of the truck cab and absently rubbed his bare finger.

"What's the matter?" Nancy asked.

"Nothing," he said quickly. "You ready?"

"Don't you need to put lotion on?"

He smirked. "Bring it. You can rub me down when we're on the water."

She laughed and rolled her eyes, but slipped the lotion in her bag.

Together, they walked out on the dock and Justin stepped onto the boat. The *Thunderbird* was his grandfather's, but it was left to Justin after he passed. He made an effort to get out on it as much as he could—twice as much if he counted his outings with Nancy too.

Justin extended his hand and helped Nancy onto the boat. They'd both been on enough times that they fell into an easy routine of disengaging from the dock, starting the engine, and slowly backing out into the water.

When they emerged into Presque Isle Bay and were far enough away from the shore and other boaters, Justin kicked up the throttle and drove out toward the Erie Harbor Channel that led to the rest of Lake Erie. Every time he took Nancy out in public he was always careful to make sure that nobody spotted them.

Not that the *Thunderbird* was a unique boat or anything.

Once they got through the channel, Justin slowed the engine. Nancy tapped him on the bare shoulder.

"Put something on before you burn," she said. "Do you want me to do it?"

"Sure." Behind his sunglasses, Justin's eyes darted back and forth to the other boats and scanned along shore too. He liked to think he was just being careful, but he knew he was really just being paranoid.

Behind him, Nancy rubbed the lotion on his shoulders, along his arms, and down his back. He obliged as much as he could while still keeping the boat in motion.

Nancy leaned over and said into his ear over the roar of the passing wind, "What's your rush?"

SIREN

"Want to make sure we get a good spot." Justin steered the boat around Gull Point and toward the west side of Presque Isle. There would be fewer eyes there and fewer chances of being caught.

His heart hadn't stopped racing since he took off his wedding ring.

He finally slowed the boat as they approached Budny Beach along the western shore of Presque Isle. Slowing to a crawl, he pulled in as close as he dared to the shore without getting in the way of anyone else. It would be easier to swim in shallower water. And if they were swimming, there would be less of a chance of someone spotting him.

Nancy pulled off her T-shirt once Justin cut the engine and stood in a tiny pink bikini.

"Oh wow," he said.

She smiled and turned for him, modeling. "Oh, this old thing?" She laughed and stepped to the back of the boat. "Come on, let's get in the water!"

Justin tossed his sunglasses on the seat and jumped off the side of the boat. When the cold water hit him, he finally felt his heart rate begin to return to normal. He and Nancy splashed each other—he even tried to carry her over his shoulder, but the sandy floor was just a little too deep for him to maintain his footing.

When they got tired, they both crawled back onto the boat and lay in the sun, fully embracing the heat that had been plaguing Erie for over a month now.

"Did you pack any snacks in that bag of tricks of yours?" Justin asked.

Nancy sat up and made a face. "I think so, but let me check." She got up and bent over her bag to inspect, pulling out a towel, the sunscreen, and a couple bottles of water and piling them on the seat.

Justin came up and wrapped his arms around her from behind, planting kisses along her shoulder.

She laughed. "Babe, not here."

He pulled away and leaned on the edge of the driver's seat. "But you look so—"

"Shoot!"

"What is it?"

"I know I packed some granola bars, but I must've left them in my other bag," she said. "Back in the truck. They're probably all melted!"

Justin shrugged. "So what? They're wrapped."

"Yeah," she said with a sigh, then patted her stomach. "I'm just getting kind of hungry."

"Me too," he admitted. He hoped to be able to stay out on the lake all day. Another trip back to the marina would mean more opportunity for them to be seen. But baking in the sun all day without any food didn't add up to anything good.

"Do you mind if we go back?" Nancy asked. She looked around and added, "There aren't too many boats out here.

Maybe we can get a good spot when we come back."

Justin looked toward the shore, then down at Nancy's pleading eyes. "Yeah, I suppose that's okay."

She kissed him. "Thanks babe! Can't wait to get back out here and spend more time with you!"

He couldn't keep the smile off his face as he started the boat back up and slowly backed away from the swimming area. When he was clear away, he kicked it into high gear, glancing over at Nancy as her long, wet hair blew in the wind.

As he rounded Gull Point and sped back across Thompson Bay, his ears tuned in to something that sounded absolutely beautiful. A woman's voice, singing. Somewhere along the shore. It was mesmerizing.

Who was it?

The song sounded familiar yet entirely new, all at the same time. It was almost…magical, the way it took him out of himself. He felt as if he was floating above himself and watching as he directed the boat toward the shore. As Nancy stared at him with panic. How she tried to pull him away.

All the while, the beautiful voice sang the song that completely took him in its grasp.

CHAPTER 2

So, what do you think?" Cheryl Anderson extended her arms out to showcase the location she picked out. Her salon-created blonde hair fluttered in the breeze.

Samantha stepped further onto the grass with Steven and Kathy trailing behind. "It's nice."

"Nice?" Kathy said. "Sam, this is gorgeous!"

They were on Presque Isle scouting possible wedding locations. For the ceremony, at least. Samantha was insistent on having a wedding on the water. She could picture the wedding photos in her head and she intended to make that vision a reality.

"Look, you can set up an archway here and get married with the city in the background." Cheryl moved to a spot near the water. "Or, you can shift it over there and have a more lush, green backdrop."

Samantha glanced over at her green option. It was another picnic area with a pull-off from the road that served as a makeshift parking lot. It was just like the one they stood on, where families could picnic and fish and spend a weekend. Just as she and Kathy had done when they were younger.

"Yeah…"

Steven hooked his arm around her waist. "You don't seem sure."

Cheryl stepped closer and continued to sell the location. "There's plenty of parking for guests. It's not too far into the park where people could get lost. I think this is a fantastic option."

Samantha bit her lip and looked around. The area was beautiful, but it was also littered with geese poop, interrupted by passing cars, and had the audience of other picnickers. Would they be able to have a sense of privacy on their wedding day?

Just as the thought came to her, a motor boat loudly came around the bend from the Presque Isle Marina from the other side of the peninsula. Nope. No privacy, whatsoever.

"Maybe we should keep looking," Samantha finally said.

Cheryl let out a heavy sigh, mourning her "perfect" suggestion. By time they all piled back in the car and she was behind the wheel directing them back toward the rest of the park, Cheryl seemed to forget all about her first suggestion.

"Oh, this next one is just breathtaking," she said as she

navigated the winding roads through the marshy peninsula. The open windows made it hard to hear her, but the July breeze wafting off the lake felt nice in the sunshine.

As they passed another pull-off, Cheryl waved at it. "That over there looks out across the water to where we just were. You were right to turn it down, Samantha, you wouldn't have been able to enjoy your special day without an audience from a bunch of strangers. Nope, your wedding should include only the people you invite."

Samantha looked out the window and watched as the road weaved through the park with paved bike paths and other picnic areas. For one stretch, they had a beautiful view of the city across the bay.

"This is gorgeous," Kathy said from the backseat.

Samantha nodded. Something was off with her today. She was excited to start wedding planning, but today she was just not in the mood to fill up her day with to-dos. She wanted to be able to enjoy the sunshine, like everyone else in Presque Isle seemed to be doing. Scouting for wedding locations seemed like a chore.

Cheryl pulled into a parking lot at the bend of another curve. "Now, this one is another excellent option." She parked the car and went to turn it off before she caught the look on Samantha's face. "What's the matter?"

Samantha shook her head as she looked around. At the pavilion just off the parking lot, the boat advertising tours of the bay docked nearby, and the number of people swarming along the sidewalk leading to the Perry Monument. "Not here. This isn't the right place."

"Why don't we just get out and look?" Steven suggested.

"Yeah, there are a lot of amenities here. Plenty of parking for guests, bathrooms, beautiful views."

"Beautiful views?" Samantha blurted. "Isn't that a smokestack I see over there?"

"Well, there are plenty of other views to see from out there," Cheryl countered. "If you want to get out I can show—"

"No, I'd rather just move on to the next place."

"Sam," Kathy said. "You didn't even give this a try."

"Look, Kathy, this isn't where I want to get married," Samantha snapped. "End of discussion. Now, can we please move on?"

Tension-filled silence swept over the car. Kathy glared up at her sister, not liking the person she was becoming as a bride. She looked across to Steven and could tell he had similar thoughts, but he gave a shrug that said, "What are you going to do?"

Cheryl quickly recovered from Samantha's outburst. Likely due to the fact that she was used to working with demanding brides. "Well all right then, on we go!" She put the car in drive and continued up the road through the park.

Not far down the road, Cheryl slowed and pointed. "The

Lagoon picnic area is nice, but there's not much of the view you said you wanted. We can take a look, but—"

"That's okay," Samantha said. "What else is there?"

Cheryl pulled back onto the road. "Well, I have a few more options. They'll take bit more work, but it's still manageable."

"This pull-off here has a nice view," Kathy suggested from the backseat. "Doesn't look like there's anyone here, either."

"And how many different camera angles are we going to be able to get from there?" Samantha fired back. "Besides, that's a gravel parking lot. My dress would be ruined."

Kathy bit down on her lips to hold in her retort.

"No, of course you'd want to preserve your dress as best you can," Cheryl said. "So I suppose that rules out a beach wedding?"

Samantha rocked her head back and forth. "I'd be open to that."

"Oh, super!" Cheryl turned off into a parking area that was swarming with cars and people in swimsuits and bags with sand toys.

"This isn't what I was thinking—"

Cheryl held up a finger to Samantha. Kathy and Steven smirked from the back. "Hold on before you start saying no. This place is a little bit off-the-beaten-path, if you will, but it is definitely a contender. Would certainly make for a unique wedding location!"

She kept driving away from the parking lot and along

Horseshoe Pond with the various houseboats floating on the water. They passed the Coast Guard with the barbed wire chain link fence along the road keeping trespassers out.

"Where are you taking us, Cheryl?" Steven asked.

"Just you wait a see!" she said with a smirk.

Finally, they came to the end of the road and she parked in a small lot along a concrete pier that led to a lighthouse.

"Oh," Samantha said, surprised. Both at the location and the fact that despite a hot July afternoon, there were few people out at this end. She wondered if that was just luck, though.

"Look, there are bathrooms right here," Cheryl pointed out. "Only a few parking spots, so that's something to consider. Maybe you could encourage your guests to carpool, or hire a driver. Maybe a bus or a limo."

"Easy with the expenses, Cheryl," Steven said with a chuckle.

She swatted him playfully. "Come here, you have to see the lighthouse. I thought this would be a beautiful spot for your ceremony. Or at least some pictures." She led them toward the pier as she talked. "Now, this lighthouse is old and a little rusty, but if you put enough distance from it so it's prominent, but the details can't be seen, you'll never even know the difference!"

The trio followed her onto the concrete pier and they started toward the lighthouse.

"Doesn't this pose safety concerns?" Kathy asked.

Cheryl seemed to just notice the water. "Oh yeah, well, maybe. But this view! Oh my gosh, I can't get over it! It's simply gorgeous! Honestly, Samantha, you're going to look stunning standing here in your wedding gown."

Kathy wasn't sure how practical this spot was, but Samantha seemed excited for the first time all day so she didn't burst her sister's bubble just yet. They could have their reality discussion later at home, without the presence of Cheryl egging her on.

Funny how the tables had turned and now Kathy needed to bring her sister back to reality.

Kathy leaned in closer to Steven and muttered, "Perhaps you should see if you can reel in some of Cheryl's suggestions while I try to get a feel for what's going on with your future wife?"

He nodded. "Hey, uh, Cheryl. Can I have a word?"

Kathy nudged her sister's arm as Steven stepped forward to keep walking with Cheryl. The sisters hung back long enough to put some space between them for private conversation.

"So what do you think?" Samantha fussed with her hair being whipped around in the wind. "This is pretty cool, huh?"

"Cool, yes, but not that realistic."

"What do you mean?"

"Samantha, seriously?" Kathy said. "This isn't a wedding

venue. It *might* be a place to take pictures, but even that has its challenges. The Coast Guard would never allow a wedding up here."

The hum of a motorboat droned in the distance, growing closer.

"They might make an exception," Samantha said. "With enough…*persuasion*."

"No, you're not using your magic on them and unless you suddenly came into a large sum of money to bribe them or you've thrown away all your morals about selling yourself, then you're fresh out of options."

Samantha shot her sister a look, not appreciating the jab. "What's calling this off is this damn wind." She gathered her hair once again and held it on the side of her neck. "I'm not going to pay a fortune to have my hair done only to have it *un*done in a matter of minutes out here."

The drone of the motorboat got louder as it came into view in Thompson Bay.

"And you were complaining about boats before," Kathy pointed out. "There are boats here too. And could you imagine describing how to get to this place to all of your guests?"

Samantha stared out into the water.

"Are you even listening?" Kathy asked.

"He's going awfully fast."

"Who is? What are you talking about?" Kathy rolled her eyes, frustrated.

Samantha pointed to the motorboat, who was still zooming full-speed across the bay toward the beach filled with people.

"Yeah." All annoyance evaporated out of Kathy as she noticed the man in the motorboat. "He is going fast. He needs to slow down. The waves from the boat alone could make the swimming hard for the people on the beach." On the boat beside the man was a woman tugging at his arm.

"I'm more concerned about what he's driving toward," Samantha said. "Or rather, *who*. Look." She pointed to a spot along the beach, closer to the pier. A woman stood in a lavender dress with her arm outstretched toward the driver of the boat. She was down the shore away from the swimmers on the beach, making it clear that she was the boat's destination.

"You think he's charging toward her?" Kathy asked.

"Certainly looks that way, doesn't it?" Samantha cast a look in Steven and Cheryl's direction. They were standing at the lighthouse deep in conversation, both facing toward the city, away from the charging motorboat.

"It almost looks like she's drawing him to her."

"Sure," Samantha said dismissively. "We need a spell. Fast."

"Uh, okay, give me a second."

"We don't have a second!"

"You're not helping!" Kathy watched as the boat came closer into view. The driver didn't seem to be aware of his surroundings, only his destination and getting there as quickly as possible. What he needed was a rude awakening and maybe the spray of the lake would do the trick. "Okay, repeat after me."

Together, they recited:

Magic spirits,
hear our call:
Raise the water,
build a wall.
Stop this man
from ending it all!

In a rush, the water from the shore shot up like a geyser, sucking the water from around the bay and spraying it in all directions. The man seemed to regain his rightful mind and eased up on the throttle and quickly tried to steer the boat away from the geyser and the shore. The woman in the boat beside him fell into a nearby seat and held on to the handles with a firm grip.

When the water rained back down, it created a wave that sent water splashing up along the edges of the bay, crashing against the pier and drenching the sisters in the process. The sisters clung to each other as they stumbled back, but managed to keep themselves from falling over the other side of the pier from the force of the wave. With one quick check, Kathy confirmed that nobody else had fallen into the water.

"Looks like it worked." She looked out at the bay. The water was still lapping up against the shore and the swimmers on the beach were all retreating further up the sand.

"Yeah, but now I'm soaked," Samantha complained. "Good thing it's warm today. Too bad it can't get out the stench of algae."

Steven and Cheryl hurried up the pier, both of them wet, though not as bad as the sisters.

"Are you guys okay?" he asked, taking Samantha in his arms.

"Just peachy," she said. "How are you so dry?"

"We hid behind the lighthouse," he said.

"Maybe this isn't such a good spot to have the ceremony," Cheryl said, stating the obvious.

"Let's just get back to the car and go home," Samantha said. "I want to change into dry clothes." She sniffed her arm, then added, "And take a shower."

"Come on, let's go," Cheryl ushered them back to the car. "We'll pick up the venue hunt another day."

Kathy let the rest of them pass by as she took another look out into the bay. Something about the whole situation didn't sit well with her. The man in the boat was completely out of it and the woman with him seemed to be scared. Almost as if he was under a spell. And that woman on the beach—

Kathy nearly stumbled backward when she finally spotted

the woman in the lavender dress. She was scowling in Kathy's direction, soaking wet. The way she stared at Kathy made it seem like she knew Kathy was the one who cast the spell that caused the geyser.

Turning, Kathy jogged to catch up to the others, hoping they didn't just gain an enemy they knew nothing about.

CHAPTER 3

H i, what can I get for you?" Kathy asked with a forced smile.

"Yeah, can I get a footlong hot dog, a bacon cheeseburger, and some curly fries?" A man asked, looking up at the menu above Kathy's head as he ordered. He had a nasty sunburn. At least, to Kathy it looked like he did. It was hard to tell under the array of neon lights swarming on the ceiling of the fine food establishment she had the displeasure to call "work."

"That'll come with two drinks, is that okay?"

He continued to look up at the menu as he pulled his wallet out of his khaki shorts. "Yeah, that's fine. Just Coke."

Kathy set two empty cups on a tray and nodded to the machines on the other side of the room. "You can fill them over there. Will that be all?"

"Yeah. What's the damage?"

She told him the number and took his money, fishing in the drawer to make change. She handed the coins back to him and piled his order onto the tray as it came out of the kitchen, all the while grateful that the lunch rush seemed to be dying down. Her feet were killing her, but she knew that if she leaned on the counter or looked bored, her manager would yell at her. "If you have time to lean, you have time to clean," was his motto.

"You're all set, sir," she said once the curly fries come up from the kitchen.

"Thanks," the man called over his shoulder as he headed back to his table with his wife and son.

As Kathy watched them her mind went to Samantha. That could be her in a couple years. A wife, a mother. All while Kathy was working checkout in a fast food restaurant at the entry of Presque Isle State Park. When had her life gone off the rails?

"There's my working girl."

Kathy couldn't help but smile when Jeremy leaned across the counter to give her a kiss. He often visited her at work, coming unannounced to see her in action. Always called her his "working girl" too. Although, she suspected he came so often for the curly fries.

"What are you doing here?" she asked, even though she knew the pattern. She was already ringing up his fries and fishing in the tip jar to pay the two dollar charge.

"Just thought I'd surprise you," he said.

"It wasn't at all about the fries, was it?"

He grinned. "Well, if you have any available."

"Curly fries!" someone from the back called.

Kathy reached back and handed them to Jeremy.

"Are you busy?" he asked.

She looked up at the clock. "I could probably take my break. Let me just double check with my manager."

Ten minutes later, they were sitting on the curb at the edge of the parking lot. Jeremy picked at his order of curly fries. Kathy leaned forward and did her best to hide her uniform, all the while wondering how bad she stunk like the fryers.

"You want one?" he offered.

She made a face and shook her head. "I know how that stuff is made. I'm not about to eat any of it."

Jeremy looked down at the carton as if considering if he should continue, then shrugged and reached for another fry. "So how was venue scouting with your sister this morning?"

They had dropped Kathy off at the restaurant on their way out of the park this morning. Lucky for Kathy, the restaurant's stench of the fryers was worse than her lake water shower earlier that morning.

"Meh, not great."

"Samantha didn't find anywhere she liked?"

Kathy rolled her eyes. "She was being so nit-picky. She wants an outdoor wedding, but she doesn't want to deal with other people being around or the wind or the dirty parking lot—but a beach wedding might be an option." She scoffed. "I don't know, she's just driving me nuts with this whole thing."

Jeremy laughed. "She's only been engaged for a few weeks. Why is she even looking for venues now anyway?"

"The sooner they decide on a venue, the sooner they can set the date," Kathy explained. "I guess it all has a domino effect or something."

"Oh."

"Yeah. I don't know. It's like Samantha's become a different person now that she's a *fiancée*." She exaggerated the accent on the word to further mock her sister. "It's like, you're not the first person to get married and you won't be the last. The rest of the world is still turning, so pull your head out of the clouds and pay attention to what's going on around you."

"I'm sorry," Jeremy mused. "Hopefully she'll snap out of it soon."

"I just hope she doesn't become this crazy lady once she's actually married. Or worse, she'll get disappointed because the excitement's over and she's just someone's wife."

"Have you talked to her about this?" Jeremy asked.

"No. She'll get all mad and defensive. I don't know, a part of me just thinks that I need to be patient. It's her wedding day and she has every right to be picky about it."

"Yeah, you'll get to be picky on your wedding day."

Kathy's head picks up. "Should I expect that to come soon?"

He made a face. "No. We're not ready to get married. I'm

still making up classes and you're—"

Jeremy managed to stop himself, but Kathy still understood the implication. The intended end of that sentence: *you're still working low-skilled jobs making virtually nothing.* Yet another reason to be disappointed with herself.

Was that all this was with Samantha? Jealousy that her sister had her life together while Kathy was barely treading water? Kathy would be lying if she said she wasn't at least a little disappointed that she and Jeremy weren't even close to getting married. It didn't even seem like marriage was on Jeremy's mind at all. And he had a point. They *weren't* ready.

"I guess I'm just not really happy with how things are going for me—"

"Oh shoot!" Jeremy said suddenly. "What day is it?"

"Um, Saturday?"

"Monday's the eleventh?"

"I guess so, why?"

"I have a paper due then and I haven't even started it!" He jumped to his feet. "I'm so sorry. I have to get to the library and get started. I'll see you later?"

"Sure." She rose to her feet. "Just call me."

"Okay." He tossed the empty carton in the trash. "It probably won't be until after the paper's done."

Kathy nodded, trying not to look disappointed that their thirty minute date was cut short. Worse, that she was about to pour her heart out to him and he just blew her off.

SIREN

He kissed her before walking backward toward his car, his keys jangling in his hand. "Have fun at work!"

She waved him goodbye and watched as he raced off to his car and pulled onto the busy road, back into the city, leaving her stranded in the last place she wanted to be.

CHAPTER 4

So I've been thinking," Samantha said minutes after picking up Kathy from work later that night. "I don't think I like the idea of a beach wedding, or maybe not even an outdoor wedding at all. The wind, the sand, the water—like what happened today—it's just too many question marks that are out of our control."

"Technically, the water today *was* in our control." Kathy hadn't thought much about the woman in the purple dress while she was at work, but now that Samantha reminded her of it, she couldn't help but wonder if they should be focusing on her and who she was and what she wanted.

"Whatever," Samantha said dismissively. "Then there's also the fact that there's limited parking at some of these places and giving directions and dealing with other people at the park. It's just too much. Besides, I don't want to make people go to one place for the ceremony and then a whole different place for the reception. I'd rather have it all in one place. Or at least closer."

Kathy looked out the window at the gas station on the corner where Samantha was waiting to turn left onto West 26th Street. She was only half listening. Samantha would probably change her mind a hundred times from now until the plans were actually set, so there was no sense in engaging in a conversation with her about it.

She knew she wasn't being a good sister—or a good maid of honor—but she was already tired of hearing about this wedding and for the moment, Samantha and Steven weren't planning on getting married until next summer. Kathy didn't know how she was going to put up with it all for a full year.

Kathy thought about what Jeremy said earlier, about saying something to Samantha. If this was going to stretch on for a year, something needed to be said sooner than later. "Don't you think you're going a little overboard with this?"

The light turned green and Samantha pulled forward, completing her turn. "What do you mean?"

"You've only been engaged a couple weeks and already you're obsessing over everything."

"Everything? I'm just talking about the venue! That's kind of important, Kathy."

"Yes, and what are you going to move on to after the venue is set?"

"I don't know, the dress maybe?" Samantha asked. "What's the big deal? It's my wedding. Can't I enjoy planning it? I just want to make sure I have everything the way I want it."

"You do realize it's Steven's wedding too?"

Samantha shot a look over at her sister before returning her eyes to the road. "Of course I realize that. Who do you think started all of this when he proposed?"

"At least I know who to blame," Kathy muttered.

"What's your problem?"

"Oh, now you want to talk about someone else other than yourself?"

"Don't be a bitch, Kathy."

"You're the one who's turned into bridezilla. Are you sure Steven's still going to want to marry you after becoming this control freak?"

"Hey!" Samantha waved her finger at her sister. She kept chancing looks back and forth between the road and Kathy. "Don't get mad at me because I got engaged first. It's not my fault I got my life together while you're still playing house with your boyfriend. If you're jealous, take it up with Jeremy, not with me."

"That's not—" Kathy stopped herself. She wasn't sure she would even believe the words that came out of her mouth if she said them. So instead she kept quiet.

Siren

"That's not what? Not fair? You said it yourself that you weren't sure you and Jeremy were going to last," Samantha went on. "If you've got problems in your relationship, I suggest you sort it out with him and leave me out of it. All I'm trying to do is live my life."

And all I'm trying to do is find mine, Kathy thought to herself.

CHAPTER 5

- AUGUST 1976 -

Heather stood at her usual post on the corner of Kensington Avenue and Sergeant Street in Philadelphia. She smoked her cigarette and looked up as the final train left the Huntingdon Station a couple blocks over. Between where she stood and where the station was, there were half a dozen girls dressed just like her—short tight skirt, high boots, and loads of makeup—all looking to make some money by filling the desires of men who were lonely enough to pay for fake companionship.

Unlike most of the girls, Heather tried to be a little more choosy than that. She usually went for the men who were simply bored with their lives and their wives. The ones who wanted to talk after, complain about their wives, all the while claiming that they still loved them. Heather found that if she talked to them and made her words seem genuine, the same men came back looking for her and would pay more to make sure she remained available for them.

Of course, word got out that Heather had stumbled on a way to squeeze a few extra bucks out of these guys—without drugging them and stealing from them when they were knocked out—and suddenly all the other girls on Kensington were trying to poach her regulars. Some had even succeeded in doing so. But that was the business.

Heather flicked her cigarette butt on the sidewalk and crushed it under the sole of her boot. Like anything in life, success came from persistence. As much as she hated spending her evenings trying to catch the eye of a poor sap who would take her to a fleabag motel to take advantage of her and then cry on her shoulder afterward, she knew that in order to make a living, this is what it took for people like her.

Nowadays that's what it took. When she first gave up singing at open mics, she tried busking at the Huntingdon Station instead. She figured she could make some money from people getting on and off the train.

So young.

So naïve.

The Heather back in those days didn't realize that this portion of Kensington was known for one kind of...*profession*. The oldest one, in fact. It was only a matter of time before she ditched the guitar and gave in to what the neighborhood was known for.

Not to mention, this paid so much more than open mics and busking ever did.

From down the street, Heather watched as a 1976 Chevy Impala drove along slowly. Behind the wheel, a middle-aged man looked around nervously, ashamed for showing his face in this part of town.

As if he was the first of his type.

He pulled to the curb in front of Heather and looked down at his lap.

Heather walked up and leaned into his open window. Now that she got a good look at him, she saw he was decent-looking. Not that she tried to evaluate her clients by their looks, but he stood out because he probably had most of his teeth. That was a plus in her book.

"What are you doing in this part of town, sweetheart?" she asked.

He gulped and gripped the wheel. Heather noted the wedding ring on his left hand.

"I—I—I don't know."

"Just sit here and think about it, then," she said. "I'm not going anywhere."

Finally, he turned to her and extended his hand. "I'm Dale."

"Oh, we're doing names?" She smiled to try to lighten the mood, but she'd seen men like him before. So afraid of their own shadow that anything she said to them seemed like a betrayal of their wedding vows. "I'm Heather." She leaned forward and took his hand.

He returned his hands to the steering wheel and didn't say anything else.

"Well, Dale, I'm assuming this is your first time?"

Sheepishly, he nodded.

"Would you like me to get in?" she asked.

Again, he nodded.

She stood, made eye contact with the girl across the street from her and gave her a look that said, "Haha! I got this one!"

When she was in the passenger seat of Dale's car, she patted his leg and told him, "Don't be nervous. I'll take good care of you."

CHAPTER 6

Sorry I'm late," Samantha said breathlessly as she took her seat across from Steven at Smuggler's Wharf on the pier. It was a perfect place to eat in the summer, being that it was right on the water. The rafters and beams above them in the restaurant were covered with leafy vines, giving it a tropical island feel, even in the humid Erie weather.

"It's okay." He was wearing a sharp gray dress shirt with faint squares on it. His sleeves were rolled up lazily, likely because he would probably be rolling them back down once he got back to work.

Samantha fussed with her napkin and adjusted herself in her seat. "Mr. Marsden wanted me to sort through a whole pile of forms we're being audited on but he wouldn't stop talking, even when I told him I was meeting you for lunch. And then when I got down here, finding parking was a treat." She took in a deep breath and looked at him. "But I'm here now."

"Well, I'm glad." Steven reached for his water. "So Mr. Marsden is keeping you busy?"

"He sure is." She made a face, then relaxed. "It's not that bad. I guess it's proof that he values the work I do. But it's still a small office so there's a lot of grunt work to be done by everyone. He's just as busy."

"But you like working there?"

"Oh, absolutely," she said. "I know it sounds boring, but I like getting the numbers to match and seeing spreadsheets fill up and all of that good stuff. Plus, it pays pretty well. I don't have to worry about how I'm going to pay school or city taxes."

Since the house she and Kathy lived in had long since been paid for, they didn't have a mortgage to worry about. But that meant dishing out loads of money when the taxes were due. Of course, the lack of a mortgage alleviated a monthly payment through the year when they were scrapped for cash while Samantha was working her way through college. Kathy helped when she could, but her income was never reliable.

"Well, when we're married you won't have to worry about the bills by yourself," Steven said.

"Kathy works…" Samantha felt obligated to come to her

sister's defense, but Kathy's actions spoke louder. Besides, Kathy and her were still on shaky ground from their argument two days earlier.

Steven politely smiled and changed the subject. "Have you heard from Cheryl since Saturday?"

"No, and I need to talk to her. It was on my to-do list to call her today but it doesn't look like I'm going to get to it. I'm not sure I like the idea of an outdoor wedding anymore."

"I thought you had a vision?"

"I do, but maybe we could just do pictures outside and have the ceremony and the reception all in one place," Samantha wondered aloud. "Of course, that would mean our guests would have to wait without us while we went and took pictures. Unless we kept it small and then maybe they could come too. But that would defeat the purpose of having everything in one place."

Steven put his hand on hers. "Sam, you're overthinking right now. One step at a time. We haven't even finalized a guest list."

"I know." Samantha pulled away from him and dug in her bag. "I've been putting together a few people I thought we could invite." She kept digging through all of her contents, still not finding her list. "Just some random ideas. None of this is final yet." She gave up on her bag and slumped her shoulders. "Shoot, I know I have a list somewhere. I wonder if I left it at the office."

"Well, there are a couple guest list givens that I want to talk about right now."

Samantha furrowed her brow. "I thought you said one of your friends from work would be your best man—uh, Charlie, right? And Kathy's going to be my maid of honor." The thought of that at the moment stung a little.

"I'm not talking about that," he said. "You've never officially met my parents."

"Yes, I have!"

He gave her a look. "Waving to them from the car when I dropped off one of my mom's dishes does not count."

Samantha turned her attention over Steven's shoulder out to the water and the people in shorts and tank tops passing by, enjoying the weather. She was nervous about meeting his parents, especially since she couldn't return the favor. The only family she had left was her sister, and Steven had complained numerous times that she and Kathy were sometimes too close.

"I want an official introduction," he went on. "A sit-down discussion introduction."

She couldn't help but smirk at his goofiness.

"We're going to be family," he pressed. "I want everyone to get along. That means building relationships before it's required."

"I don't know, Steven," she said. "I'm nervous. What if they don't like me? A mother is always very protective of her son. It doesn't matter if I was Mother freakin' Teresa, she's not going to like me."

"Hey, if you don't want her to make snap judgments about

you, don't tarnish her image in your mind before you even give her a chance."

Samantha looked down at the menu in front of her. She hadn't even opened it yet.

Steven had a point. She needed to give his parents—his mother, specifically—a chance before any assumptions were made. This woman was going to be her mother-in-law. Maybe she could help fill the mother void that Samantha had been missing for so long.

"Okay. I'll give it a try," Samantha finally said. "But your mother's not going to want to plan the wedding, is she?"

Steven shrugged. "It probably wouldn't hurt to invite her to some things."

She shot him a look.

"Like the dress fitting or cake tasting or even the venue scouting we've been doing. It's just an idea. Like I said, it'd help you build a relationship with her."

Samantha huffed and then realized how childish and controlling she was being. "Okay. I suppose I can do that."

He smiled. "Thanks."

She reached across the table and squeezed his hand.

"While we're meeting parents, if you wanted to call your dad and—"

She pulled away and let out an annoyed sigh. "Steven, no. My dad left us five years ago to *find himself*. We haven't heard from him since so he must've figured out who he was and that doesn't involve us anymore."

"You don't know that," he countered. "For all you know he could be waiting for you to—" Steven stopped mid-sentence and picked his head up, turning toward the pier.

"Steven?"

He stood and walked to the exit.

"Steven, where are you going?" Samantha called after him, but he ignored her and kept walking, further onto the pier.

Grumbling, Samantha grabbed her bag and Steven's wallet sitting on the table and followed him out the door.

CHAPTER 7

teven!" Samantha called to her fiancé as she exited the restaurant. Several people in the area looked at her as she called after him, so she adjusted the strap of her bag on her shoulder and picked up her speed to catch up to him.

He continued to march further down the pier, without even a look back in her direction.

Power-walking to keep up with him without drawing attention to herself, Samantha was grateful that the crowd thinned the closer they got to the end of the pier. But then, she began to fear that he would eventually step right off and into the water.

As she left the hubbub of the crowd behind, a hauntingly beautiful song carried through the air. She couldn't place exactly where it was coming from, but it made her want to follow it. To seek out its source. The song only got louder and more intense as she followed Steven, nearly forgetting why her feet were carrying her in this direction in the first place.

Finally, Steven came to an abrupt stop near the end of the pier and Samantha collided with him since she was so consumed by the song. Jolting into him pulled her out of her head and she was startled to see a woman with long dark hair and a flowing light purple dress stranding in front of them with a sinister smirk. She looked familiar, but Samantha couldn't quite remember from where.

Samantha hooked one of her arms possessively around one of Steven's. At least this way he wouldn't go any further.

"Men can't resist my song," the woman said.

"Steven, look at me," Samantha pleaded. He continued to stare straight again. She tried again, this time pushing her persuasion power to him. "Steven, I said look at me."

Still nothing.

Turning to the woman, Samantha asked, "Who are you?"

"You don't remember? Perhaps it's because I'm dry. Maybe if I was drenched in lake water it'd jog your memory."

Samantha suddenly remembered. "You're the woman from the beach the other day. The one who was trying to make that man in the boat crash."

"He was simply answering my call," she said defiantly. "If the love of his life couldn't protect him—or his mistress—then that was their fault and not mine."

"Well, luckily we were there," Samantha said. "Who are you? What's your name? What do you want?"

The woman stepped forward and ran the back of her hand along Steven's cheek, who leaned into it, much to Samantha's horror. "My name's Heather. And you and your…sister, is it?"

Samantha followed Heather's every move closely with her eyes, but offered no response.

"You interrupted me from fulfilling my life's purpose."

"Your life's purpose?" Samantha asked. "Killing men is your life's purpose?"

Heather squeezed Steven's hand. "Does he look dead to you? On the contrary, he looks very much alive."

"Stop touching him!" Samantha snapped.

Heather quickly drew her arms back to herself and stared at Samantha with wonder. "Oh, does that upset you?"

"Why wouldn't you groping him upset me? He's my fiancé!"

The woman smiled. "Ah, I see. Your passion is still very much alive. The monotony of life hasn't beaten it out of you. He hasn't had a chance to let his eyes wander and betray you."

"He wouldn't betray me," Samantha said. "That's why I'm marrying him. And I don't have to justify or defend my relationship to you."

"Yes, because you're a *strong, independent* woman," she said mockingly.

"What's that supposed to mean?"

Heather smirked and looked Steven up and down. "Perhaps he deserves someone who could be more attentive to his…needs."

Frustrated, Samantha decided not to continue this back and forth anymore. "Look, I'm getting tired of all of this. I just need you to take off whatever spell you have him under."

"Spell? What spell?"

"You know what I mean," she said through gritted teeth.

"I assure you there is no spell on your lover," Heather said. "I can't help it that he's drawn to me and my song."

Samantha took a step forward, careful to keep one hand on Steven's arm. "I don't know what you're playing at, but you need to stop it! You're mad at us for stopping you from killing a man. I'm not going to apologize for saving him. So why don't you go back to whatever cave you crawled out of and leave us the hell alone."

Heather raised her eyebrows but looked otherwise unperturbed. "So feisty. No, I won't leave you alone. You see, I might not have an effect on you—at least, not as strong as I'd like—but I do have an effect on your lover. And I'm assuming your sister has someone special in her life too?" She scoffed. "Oh, of course she does. A beautiful woman such as her doesn't stay single for long!"

"What's your point? Why is it such a big deal that we stopped you from leading that man to his death?"

"I told you, it's my life's work. Punishing men for their

uncontrollable temptations. Honestly, it's really a service to women, protecting them from inevitable heartbreak."

"How do you know these men even cause heartbreak?"

Heather snickered. "All men do! The ones who hear my song first are the guiltiest."

"Then why didn't anyone else come when you sang your song just now?"

"That one was just for him." She leaned up and patted Steven's cheek.

"Stop touching him!"

"He seems to like it."

And he did. Steven leaned into Heather's palm, eyes closed, enjoying every moment of the attention he was receiving from her, even though he was otherwise oblivious to everything else around him. Envy boiled inside Samantha. She knew it was only a spell or some other type of magic.

"What do we need to do to get you to leave us alone?" Samantha asked as a way to distract Heather from Steven.

"Oh, what you've done can't be undone," she said. "No, now it's time for you and your sister to pay the price—and that may just cost you your men."

"But they didn't do anything wrong!"

"Not yet," Heather said with a smirk. "Well, I wish I could stay and chat, but I have business to attend to." She leaned up and gave Steven a kiss on the cheek.

Samantha reached for her to push her away from Steven,

but Heather was too quick and pulled away, out of Samantha's reach.

"We will mostly certainly be seeing more of each other." Heather gave Steven another once-over. "At least, he and I will be. Mmm, can't wait."

Heather left them and continued down the pier back into the city. Spinning around, Samantha let go of her hold on Steven to chase after her, but she was gone. It was like she vanished into thin air.

The magic Heather had on Steven broke and he groaned seconds before crumbling to the ground.

"Steven!" Samantha knelt to his side and checked to make sure he didn't hit his head. "Are you okay?"

He sat up slowly. "Samantha? How did we—why am I on the ground?"

"Are you hurt?"

He shook his head and looked at the few other people on the pier, then began to rise to his feet.

Samantha helped him up. "Are you sure you're okay?"

"I'm fine. What happened? I didn't have a drink with lunch, did I? Last thing I remember we were talking about your parents."

As grateful as she was to have escaped that conversation, Samantha would have had it a million times over if it meant that Heather hadn't put her spell on Steven.

Instead of answering him—since she was drawing a blank

on a possible explanation—Samantha helped him swat off dirt and dust from the back of his pants.

"So you don't remember walking down here?"

"Not at all. Did we finish lunch early and go for a walk? What time is it now?" He checked his watch. "Shoot, I'm running late."

They turned and headed back to where they each parked, the whole time Samantha looked around for any sign of Heather. There was none. The fact that Steven didn't remember anything was good, but it still left a lot of questions to be answered. Chief among them: who exactly was Heather and what did she want?

CHAPTER 8

Heather watched as the Chevy Impala drove up Kensington Avenue again. She smiled. She wasn't sure Dale would be back for another round. He was so nervous when she picked him up last month that she didn't think she'd ever see him again, which was a shame. He was a big tipper. Must've been the guilt.

After stubbing out her cigarette, she took one step forward toward where he parked in an empty spot several feet away. But she stopped when she saw Jessica nearly run to his door.

Despite Heather remaining tight-lipped about how much Dale paid her, word spread quick that he was generous. It was a hazard of rooming with women in the same profession. Couldn't trust anybody.

Resigning herself to defeat, Heather returned to her spot on the corner and fished in her top for her cigarettes, but stopped when she heard Jessica call out.

"Fine, asshole! Your loss!" She stalked back to her post and crossed her arms with a puss on her face.

Heather knew their pimp would be around soon. It wasn't good for business to see a car waiting for too long. Heather and the other girls were told that they needed to move quick, practically throw themselves in men's cars just to keep "business booming."

Easy for someone like him to say, who didn't have to be alone with some of these creeps.

Heather watched as the Impala pulled away from the curb. She was surprised that she felt almost saddened by it. Dale might've been nervous and guilty, but he was sweet. She didn't see that a lot from most of the men who came to this street looking for a little action.

No longer craving a cigarette, Heather pressed the pack back into her cleavage, openly fixing herself on the street. If anything, it was good for business to be unafraid of a little public groping. At least this time she was only doing it to herself.

The sound of an engine coming up Sergeant Street startled her. When she turned to look in that direction, a smile came across her face.

It was the Impala.

Siren

"You busy tonight?" he asked her through the open window.

"I'm open for you, sweetheart." She strode confidently toward him, knowing that Jessica was probably watching her with dismay. Heather was in for a "discussion" with the pimp tomorrow, but she wasn't afraid of him. She was afraid of starving to death so she needed to do what she needed to do to keep food in her belly.

"I really enjoyed being with you before," he said once she was at the window. "This is the first time I've been able to get away since."

"I was hoping you'd show up around here again soon," Heather told him.

Dale looked down in his lap and smiled bashfully. "Why don't you hop in then?"

His words were confident, but his body language still gave off the impression of a high school freshman asking a girl out for the first time. Heather thought it was cute and she got in.

As they drove past Jessica, Heather waved at her but only got the middle finger in return.

It was tough out on the streets.

CHAPTER 9

After spending another long shift working amidst greasy food and rude customers, the last place Kathy wanted to be was another diner. Luckily she at least had the sense to change out of her uniform before Jeremy picked her up to take her to the diner in Lawrence Park. It was a place he and his friends visited frequently since it was just around the corner from his house and right on Main Street in the borough.

"There you guys are!" Maddie said from a booth in the corner. She was dating Jeremy's roommate Michael and the two of them were squished into one side of the booth.

"We were beginning to think you guys weren't coming," Paul said from the other side of the booth. He craned his head to look around his girlfriend Becky, who was seated beside him.

"Yeah, sorry," Jeremy said as he and Kathy walked up. "I had to pick up this one from work all the way over near Presque Isle."

The rest of the group tried to make room on the small table. Maddie even tried to squeeze closer to Michael to give the newcomers a place to sit. Instead, Jeremy just pulled up two chairs and he and Kathy sat at the end.

"Oh yeah," Becky said. "How do you like working there?"

Kathy shrugged. "It's okay, I guess. Better than not having a job, but it's a tourist area, so…"

"Could you get us free food?" Paul asked. Becky smacked him. "What?" he asked her. "I'm saving for a house. I need to cut as many corners as I can!"

Paul was staying with Jeremy and Michael for a few months because the rent was cheaper than his other apartment downtown. There wasn't a definite move-out date for him, but he claimed he wanted to be into his own house by the spring, so it would only be for less than a year.

Of course, that meant that Becky was over at the apartment all the time too. On the few nights all three guys and their girlfriends stayed over, it made for a packed house. And it wasn't that big of a house to begin with.

"No, I don't make the food," Kathy said.

"Too bad. We would've made the drive out there for free food."

Thankfully I don't have to spend another minute longer there than I have to, Kathy thought to herself.

"I'm starving," Jeremy said, sensing that Kathy wanted the attention off of her. He waved toward Michael. "Hand me one of those menus."

"Oh, we already ordered for you guys," Maddie said.

"How'd you know what we wanted?" Jeremy asked.

Michael rolled his eyes. "You want breakfast, so we ordered you a large stack of pancakes. And Kathy, we got you a turkey club with chips, not fries. Your usual."

She smiled. "Thanks."

"Oh, and here it comes!" Becky cheered as the waitress walked up.

Margaret, who had been their waitress several times before, balanced a large tray on her shoulder until she reached them. She set the tray down on a nearby table and started passing out the baskets of food.

"Is there anything else I can get you?" she asked. She had a pencil tucked behind one ear and a cigarette in the other.

"No, thank you," Kathy said with a smile.

The group began to dig into their food. Since Jeremy and Kathy were on the end, they didn't have room to properly pull close to the table to eat comfortably. That meant Kathy held the basket under her as she ate and Jeremy sloppily cut into his pancakes on the edge of the table.

The bell over the door rang as a woman with dark hair stepped in. She wore a flowy lavender sundress and Kathy did a double take as she realized that she had seen this woman before.

The one from the beach.

The one who tried to lead a man in a boat toward shore.

The one Kathy and Samantha had cast a spell to stop only a few days earlier.

The woman took a seat at a table and reached for a menu. She gave a sinister look up to Kathy before redirecting her eyes to the menu. Softly, she began to hum to herself and yet, the sound seemed to carry across the diner.

"Guys, check her out," Michael said.

Jeremy and Paul both looked over at the woman.

"Damn," Paul said.

"Really?" Maddie asked. "We're all sitting right here. Are you really checking out another girl?"

"What?" Michael asked. "Is it so bad to look?"

"Just let the poor girl eat in peace," Becky said.

"We're not bothering her," Paul countered. "Jeremy, back me up on this."

He put up his free hand. "Hey, I'm too smart to have a wandering eye when I have the most attractive girl right here." He leaned over to give Kathy a sticky kiss. She couldn't help but laugh as she pushed him away.

"So how's summer school going?" Becky asked Jeremy.

"It's not summer school," he started before he dove into how he was getting into a routine with the schoolwork, even though he nearly forgot to write the paper that was due first thing in the morning.

With her sandwich gone, Kathy picked at her chips and glanced in the woman's direction while trying to look casual. She didn't like that the woman was there. Clearly it was because Kathy was there, which made her nervous. The woman wouldn't try anything with all of these innocent people here as witnesses, would she?

"Michael, cut it out," Maddie said, pulling Kathy's attention back to the table. "Paul, you too. Leave her alone. Jeremy is managing."

Kathy noticed that Jeremy's plate was nearly empty while the other two boys still had most of their food left. They kept stealing glances at the woman from the beach.

"If you guys are like this when we're sitting right here, how are you when we're not?" Becky asked. "Seriously, this is annoying." She grabbed ahold of Paul's chin and redirected his head back to the table. "Enjoy the company you're with, will you?"

Maddie swatted at Michael. "You too. Cut it out."

Kathy looked over at her boyfriend. He seemed more interested in his dwindling stack of pancakes than the woman.

At least I don't have to worry about him having a wandering eye, she thought.

But the woman's humming was audible from across the restaurant. Even verging on loud. At least, that's the way it felt to Kathy. No one else seemed bothered. Well, except for Michael and Paul who seemed to have other things on their mind.

"Excuse me," Paul said to Becky, who was blocking him in.

"What?" she asked.

"I need to use the bathroom."

"Not if you're going to bother that poor girl."

He made a face. "Come on, you can trust me. Besides, a friendly smile won't hurt anything."

"Paul, don't," Kathy said to him. "Just…leave her alone."

"Yeah, don't be stupid," Maddie added. "Just walk right by her without doing anything."

"I will. I promise. Now move." Paul nudged Becky and she finally relented, sliding out of the booth, scooting around Kathy's seat so he could get out.

"I think I need to pee too," Michael said, no longer trying to hide the fact that he was now staring at the woman.

"No, Paul doesn't need any help," Maddie said. "You can stay put."

"But—"

She grabbed his arm and gave him a stern look. "Seriously, you're embarrassing me. You think you can control yourself for two minutes? I'm about to pack up and leave because you're so frustrating."

Michael squirmed in Maddie's grip and glanced over in the woman's direction briefly, then completely. "I know, but—she's gone!"

CHAPTER 10

Like a charm, Heather's song brought the boy willingly. The only thing she was worried about was getting out of the restaurant without the rest of his group seeing. Luckily, there were so many of them to create a distraction that that hadn't been a problem.

"This way, sweetheart," Heather said to the boy as she led him along the sidewalk in front of the diner and to the side alley between the diner and the neighboring building.

Without a word, he followed, completely in a trance. He wasn't her original target, but she was going to take what she could get. It would still send a message and cause at least one of the witches some hurt. Maybe even serve as a stepping stone to get to her true target: the witch's boyfriend.

SIREN

At the back of the alley, Heather reached for the boy's hands. She smiled when she saw him further melt to her touch. She loved having that power over men. This one was no different than every other man she encountered: he had a wandering eye and was willing to cross the line and betray the woman he was committed to.

Her magic wouldn't have worked if he wasn't in love with his girl.

"It's just you and me now," she told him. "Are you sure you want to do this?"

Always important to ask for consent, even if his answer was magically influenced.

The boy looked at her with hunger in his eyes and nodded. He stood slack-jawed and seemed empty of his thoughts. Like putty in her hands.

"I noticed you were with that girl in there," Heather said. "You love her, don't you?"

The confirmation of that was icing on the cake for her.

Again, he nodded without a word.

"But you still want to kiss me?"

Another nod.

"Well, if you're willing to risk it all, I suppose there's nothing I can do to stop you," she said coyly. "I tend to have that effect on a lot of guys."

The boy leaned forward, as did Heather. When their lips touched, he began to pull away as smoke permeated from his mouth.

Instead, Heather reached around and held the back of his head to hold the kiss longer. Another moment later, she backed away as flames erupted from his mouth just before he collapsed on the ground, unmoving.

Heather wiped at her lips and cast one last look at him before walking away.

CHAPTER 11

Everyone at the table in the diner turned to look to where the woman was sitting.

"Maybe you creeped her out with all of your staring," Becky said.

"Or maybe Paul got to her first," Jeremy added.

Maddie and Becky both shot daggers at him.

Kathy put her hand on Jeremy's shoulder as a horrible thought came to her. "Go check on Paul in the bathroom," she told him.

"What? I'm not—"

"Just *go!*" she told him firmly. "I want to make sure he's in there."

Everyone looked at her with a confused look, but she didn't

care. She was too worried about where Paul had gone.

"Fine, all right." Jeremy stalked off to the bathroom.

Kathy spun in her seat and looked around, trying her best to see out the windows but she couldn't see anyone outside.

"Kathy, what is it?" Maddie asked.

"Yeah, you're scaring me," Becky added.

Michael looked out the window beside him. "Do you think Paul left with her?"

Jeremy came back with a similar look of worry. "Paul's not in the bathroom."

Kathy got to her feet and rushed to the door. She could hear the rest of the group following her out and she wished they wouldn't, but she was too focused to object.

Outside, she glanced up and down Main Street, hoping to see any sign of Paul or the woman in the purple dress. But too much time had passed. They could've been anywhere, whether on foot or by car.

"Mike, you and Maddie go back to the house," Jeremy ordered. "See if Paul went back there."

"You think he took her back to—" Becky choked back tears.

Kathy stepped toward the nearest corner, where Main met Sillman Avenue.

"That's not what I'm saying," Jeremy said. "We don't know anything yet."

Before she even got to the intersection, she peered down the small alleyway between the diner and the neighboring building and saw something that made her stomach drop. Paul lay on the gravel at the back of the alley.

Kathy didn't announce her discovery, but ran to close the space between herself and his body. The others took notice and followed her.

"Oh God!" Maddie shouted behind her.

Lying on his back on the stone driveway, Paul stared up at the sky with a blank expression. His eyes were frozen open. Worst of all was the black soot covering his open mouth and his face around it. As if he was breathing in fire.

When Becky came around the guys and got a good look for herself, she let out an ear-splitting scream as the pain rocketed through her.

CHAPTER 12

ow long before you noticed he was missing?" the patrol
officer asked Kathy.

The police had everyone in their group separated as
they were each questioned. Kathy stood in the parking lot
across the street from the diner as a patrol officer took her
statement. She could see Jeremy and his friends scattered
around the area, each giving their own statements about what
happened.

"Not that long, I guess," she said, trying to focus her eyes
on the officer talking to her. Instead, her eyes kept wandering
to everyone else.

Jeremy looked pensive as he recounted the events. Michael
kept covering his mouth and wiping his face, likely fighting

back tears until he had privacy. Maddie continued to shake her head, as if in disbelief that they had found Paul dead like that. And Becky, poor Becky, was inconsolably sobbing as a female officer tried to comfort her.

Meanwhile, across the street, several other officers tended to Paul's body. Out of the corner of her eye, Kathy could see them moving around, but she tried not to make it look like she was staring.

"And what did you do when you noticed he was missing?" the officer asked.

Kathy crossed her arms and let out a deep breath. "Um…I had Jeremy check the bathroom for him and Michael was looking through the windows into the parking lot."

"You felt like he was in danger?"

She shook her head. "Not exactly, no. Um…" She hesitated. She didn't want to bring up the woman in the dress and have the police chase after her and potentially even put themselves in danger. From the little Kathy knew about this woman, one thing was clear: men seemed to be her targets. From the man on the boat to Paul—and even Michael.

But there was no way to completely eliminate the woman from the story without raising suspicion. So Kathy decided to be vague.

"I didn't want to say anything because his girlfriend is over there, but this woman walked into the diner and Paul kept making eyes at her."

"Do you think he knew her?" the officer asked.

"I don't think so, no," Kathy said. "But it was clear he liked what he saw."

"How so?"

"He kept looking at her, smiling, even made a comment, like, 'Hey, check her out' to the other guys."

"So you think he left with her?"

Kathy shrugged. "I don't know. All I know is he said he was going to the bathroom, shortly after that, we noticed the woman wasn't there. When Paul seemed to be gone a while, we looked around and that's when we found him."

The officer nodded and slipped his notepad back into the pocket of his shirt. "Okay. I have your contact information in case we need to get in touch with you again for further questions, but I think that'll do it for now. Thank you."

Kathy gave him a tight-lipped smile and walked over to Jeremy, who was finishing up with his statement.

"How'd it go?" he asked, pulling her in for a hug.

She leaned into him as he squeezed her tight. "Not bad. How are you holding up?"

He looked toward the diner and swallowed hard. "I think I just want to get home."

"Okay, I'll call Samantha and see if she can come pick me up—"

"No, I want you to stay with me," he said, then added quickly, "for your own protection. Something happened to

Paul—someone hurt him. I don't want anyone to hurt you too."

She looked into his eyes and could see fear in them, but also sadness. He needed her to stay with him more than he wanted to protect her. He was just too proud to admit it.

"Okay. Let's get you home then."

As they turned to head back home, they noticed Michael and Maddie walking up with somber looks. Maddie had her arm around her boyfriend and continued to look up at him as if to check on him.

"We're heading home," Jeremy told them. "Kathy's staying over."

"Where's Becky?" Kathy asked. She felt Jeremy slip his hand into hers, likely because he noticed Michael and Maddie's embrace.

"She's waiting with an officer until her parents pick her up," Maddie said. "She still hasn't really calmed down and the police are insisting on a statement from her."

"Should we stay with her?" Jeremy asked.

"The police wouldn't really let us talk to her," Maddie said. "She waved to us and told us to go ahead."

"Yeah, her parents live right around the corner anyway," Michael added.

Jeremy nodded and they were all silent again.

"Let's, uh, head back home," Kathy suggested.

Slowly, they all turned in the direction of Jeremy's house and started the quiet journey. As they rounded the first corner, they each took one last glance back at the diner and the horrors that would forever scar their usual hangout filled their minds.

CHAPTER 13

Kathy sat by herself on the couch in Jeremy's small living room with a cup of tea. She watched as the steam rose and disappeared into the air. She wondered if that's what happened to Paul's soul as he died. Drifted up and disappeared.

She had seen other people die before—worse deaths than Paul's. Her mind flashed back to the harpies snatching up Jeffrey Jackson while his wife screamed for him from the ground. She shivered at the thought.

Even though she hadn't actually seen Paul die, and that she didn't know him very well, she knew his death would stick with her for a while. She felt somewhat responsible for his passing. Perhaps because she knew the mysterious woman was trouble and she didn't go to lengths to protect him. She didn't even keep as close an eye on the woman as she should've. And now a man was dead.

Someone Jeremy cared for a lot, by the way he broke down once they were in the privacy of his bedroom. It was as if the closing door to his room gave him permission to open up. Kathy laid with him as he speculated, cried, got angry. With every emotion he felt, she was there to walk him through it. It took him a long time to calm down enough to fall asleep. And by then she needed an escape from the misery.

"Can't sleep?" Maddie's voice pulled Kathy out of her head.

"Huh?" Kathy hadn't heard her come down the stairs. "Oh, no. Not tired yet."

Maddie curled up on a nearby chair. She pulled a thin sweater tighter around herself. "Me neither. The worst part for me is seeing how this is affecting the guys."

Kathy nodded. "Was Michael crying too?"

"Yeah. I've never seen him like that."

"Guess it goes to show that even tough guys have feelings." Kathy raised her tea to her mouth and took a sip. "Too bad someone needed to die to show that, though."

"I know," Maddie said. "What do you think happened to him?"

Kathy shrugged. "I don't know. That's up to the police to figure out. Our job is to help the guys through it."

"Yeah, I suppose you're right." Maddie stared down at the green shag rug that had seen better days. "I can't help but feel like that girl had something to do with it."

"The woman in the purple dress?" Kathy asked and immediately regretted it. She didn't want to seem too eager to throw out a scenario. That would give the impression that she knew more than she was supposed to.

"So you were thinking the same thing too?"

Kathy looked down at her tea. The steam had faded, although the cup still kept her hands warm. "She was hard to miss."

"The whole thing about her was just weird," Maddie said. "First, the fact that she was there alone. How many people our age eat alone?"

Kathy thought the woman looked a little older than their age, but she let Maddie talk.

"And second, she was very obviously leading the guys on," she continued. "The flirty eyes, the humming—"

"You heard that too?"

"Yeah, I mean it wasn't that loud, but I definitely heard it," Maddie said. "She probably wanted the guys to hear her deep, sultry, *sexy* voice." She groaned. "Ugh, it's disgusting."

Kathy knew that Maddie was probably just projecting her feelings about what they experienced tonight onto the woman, but the fact that she heard the humming too was something. Kathy definitely thought it was quite a bit louder than "not that loud," but perhaps because she was a witch she was more prone to things like that. After all, they already knew the woman was magical by what they saw over the weekend on Presque Isle. And the fact that Paul didn't die of natural causes confirmed that.

"And then she just up and left *right* before we found Paul," Maddie went on. Her voice finally betrayed how she was really feeling. "It's not fair. Who is she and why did she want to hurt him?" She looked down and covered her eyes to keep Kathy from seeing her cry.

Kathy respected Maddie's privacy and let the girl cry for a minute, pretending not to notice. She took another sip of her tea while Maddie regained her composure.

"I'm sorry," Maddie finally said, rising to her feet. "I'm probably just emotional because I'm tired. I should go to bed."

"It's okay. We're all shook up from it," Kathy said. "If you need a friend, let me know."

Maddie offered her a sad smile and then disappeared up the stairs to Michael's room.

Kathy sat where she was until she heard Michael's bedroom door close. Then she downed her tea, got to her feet, and stepped into the kitchen for the phone. It was going on midnight, but she knew Samantha would answer. Despite whatever arguments the sisters were having, they were always able to put their differences aside when it came to magical threats.

Kathy didn't want to see someone else die because of this woman.

CHAPTER 14

Samantha stirred amongst the tangle of sheets when she heard the phone ringing downstairs. She had just started to drift off. It was one of the consequences of having Steven sleep over. She would have to get used to sharing her bed once they were married. Especially in the summer when their combined body heat created an oven box out of her bedroom.

After carefully untangling herself from the covers so she didn't wake him, she set her feet on the hardwood floor, which was mercifully cool, and slowly crept out of the bedroom and down the creaky stairs to the kitchen. All the while, she wondered who would be calling so late at night. Then she remembered as she passed her sister's room that Kathy hadn't come home.

Samantha hoped nothing bad had happened. But then, a phone call in the middle of the night was never a good thing.

The phone was almost on its last ring when she picked it up.

"Hello?"

"Sam?"

"Kathy?"

"Yeah, it's me."

"Why are you calling so late?" Samantha asked. "Where are you?"

"I'm at Jeremy's," she said. "Sorry. Were you sleeping?"

"Of course I was sleeping! It's"—Samantha turned and looked at the clock on the wall in the dark kitchen—"just after midnight. What do you need? You could've at least told me you were staying at Jeremy's."

"I hadn't planned on it," Kathy said. "But something happened."

Samantha stood up straighter, all the sleepiness drained from her mind. "Are you okay? Are you hurt?"

"I'm fine," Kathy assured her. "But I saw the woman from the beach again. The one who seemed to be calling that man in the boat to her?"

Samantha's mind went right to her own encounter with the woman during her lunch with Steven. It was the reason she insisted he spend the night. The fact that Kathy didn't come home only sealed the deal for him.

"Yeah, I remember. Did you talk to her?" Samantha said.

SIREN

The fact that Heather had talked to both sisters in the same day was enough to consider her a threat and that they were her targets.

"No," Kathy said. "We were all hanging out at the diner. Me, Jeremy, and his friends."

Samantha knew the diner. She had picked up and dropped off Kathy there on more than one occasion. Although she had never officially gone inside, she could guess what the atmosphere was like.

"We were just hanging out, eating dinner, and talking," Kathy went on. "And then the woman showed up—"

"Heather."

"What?"

"That's her name."

"How do you—"

"I saw her today too," Samantha said. "I'll explain in a bit. But first, you were saying?"

"Okay, so *Heather* showed up and at first she was just sitting there and then I heard her humming to herself, but it was pretty loud—I mean, I guess Maddie said it wasn't that loud, but the guys definitely took note. Well, Jeremy was more focused on his food than he was Heather, but that might've been because I was sitting right there."

"So what happened?"

"Jeremy's friends Michael and Paul were *really* into her. Kept looking back at her, talking about her, staring at her. It got to the point where it was a little creepy, especially with their girlfriends sitting right there telling them to stop."

"So he seemed to be transfixed on her?" Samantha asked, thinking back to the way Steven acted.

"Yeah, I guess so," Kathy said. "Kind of like the guy in the boat was on Saturday. All while the girl with him seemed oblivious."

"Right." Samantha slunk down to the floor and leaned against the wall as she talked. The cord from the phone pulled taut.

"Anyway, so Paul said he was going to go to the bathroom."

"Okay…"

"We didn't really think much of it, but then we noticed the woman was gone—Heather. And then I realized Paul had been gone for a while too."

"Did he go with her?"

Samantha could hear Kathy take a deep breath before she continued. "He must've," she said in a small voice. "I started to panic and I went outside and I found him."

"Dead?"

There was silence on the other end and then Kathy said even quieter, "Yeah. He had, uh, soot marks all around his face. As if his mouth had been on fire or something. I don't know. It was weird."

"Did you see where she went?"

"No. Jeremy and his friends all followed me out and when

they saw him, Becky, Paul's girlfriend, started screaming and Maddie called 9-1-1 and then the police came and I didn't have a chance to look for her."

"Damn. It would've been nice to see where she went."

"I kind of needed to take care of my friends first."

"Right, no," Samantha said. "You did the right thing. I just wish—well, I wish it didn't happen. Do you have any idea what we're looking at?"

"You mean what Heather is?" Kathy asked. "No. I mean, maybe she's a witch, but to be able to entice men *and* burn them alive? That doesn't sound like a witch to me. Witches usually only have one specialty and their powers grow from that specialty."

"Unless she's working with someone else," Samantha considered aloud. "That could explain how she always gets away so fast. And it could explain the firepower. Maybe Heather only lures them out so her partner could get them alone and kill them."

"But for what purpose?" Kathy asked. "The job of witches is to protect people. Save them from supernatural enemies. What kind of witch goes around killing people?"

"Evil ones."

"Maybe, but it still doesn't make sense to me," Kathy said. "I mean, we weren't even on Heather's radar until we stopped that man in the boat on Saturday. It wasn't until after that that she started targeting us. I didn't see anyone else with her, did you?"

Samantha looked down and smoothed out the wrinkles in her pajama pants. "I wasn't really paying attention." She hated to admit when she was wrong, but the truth was she wasn't in a great frame of mind on Saturday. She was ashamed to admit but she was so consumed with the wedding and finding a good venue that stopping a man from driving right onto shore seemed more like a nuisance to her than anything else.

"I'm just saying it's unlikely," Kathy said. "Did you see her with anyone else when you ran into her today? How did that happen? Where were you?"

"Steven and I were at lunch," Samantha said. "At Smuggler's Wharf."

"So apparently Heather's not afraid to strike in crowds or restaurants," Kathy said. "Maybe she uses it as protection because she knows we won't do anything to her in a public place."

"Maybe, but she lured Steven out of the restaurant."

"She targeted him specifically?"

"Must've," Samantha said. "I heard the song, but I ignored it. Steven couldn't. He was completely in a trance. I didn't like it."

"What did he do? How did you break him of it?"

"He just started walking to the end of the pier, where Heather was waiting."

"What did she do?" Kathy asked.

"She was very possessive of him," Samantha said. "Touching him, kissing his cheek."

"Do you think he's sleeping with her?"

Samantha rolled her eyes, glad that Kathy couldn't see it. "No, of course not. I think she's a seductress. Someone who tries to lure men to cheat to tarnish their relationships or, in Paul's case, kill them."

"Yeah," Kathy murmured.

"Luckily, I followed Steven out and stopped him before she could do anything to him. And I talked to her."

"What did she say?"

"Well, that's how I learned her name is Heather," Samantha said. "The whole thing just seemed like a warning for us. She mentioned that she would go after Jeremy too. I tried calling his house earlier but nobody was home and he doesn't have an answering machine so it just kept ringing."

"Oh, right. Maybe if I had gotten that call—"

"You can't blame yourself for what happened to Paul," Samantha said. "You did the best you could with what you had to work with. Now we know more about her and we'll be able to stop her—or them—next time."

"Well, now that we know for sure that they're going after our guys, I think we should keep them close," Kathy suggested. "After Paul, Jeremy wanted me to spend the night so I'm here for tonight."

"Good. And Steven's staying over tonight too."

"Well, at least that's one night down that we can be sure nothing happens to them," Kathy said. "I'm going to try to get

Jeremy to stay at our house tomorrow. If Heather's coming after Jeremy and Steven because of us, I don't want Michael or Maddie or anyone else to get hurt in Heather's vendetta to get to us."

"Good thinking," Samantha said. "I just wish there was a way to keep an eye on Steven while he's at work, but I don't think Heather would go after him at work. Since we both saw her today when we were with them, she must want us to see our men meet their demise."

"At least that makes me feel a little better about having to go into work tomorrow," Kathy said. "Hopefully I can get Jeremy up early enough to get me there."

"Yeah, that'd be way out of the way for me to come pick you up and take you," Samantha said. "Not to mention there wouldn't even be enough time."

"Yeah. We'll just have to stay on our toes. Do you think you can check *The Art of Magic* for any entries that might tell us what Heather is? Maybe if we figure that out we can put together a better plan to stop her."

"That's a good idea," Samantha said. "I'll try to look first thing tomorrow morning, but with Steven here I make no promises."

Kathy was quiet for a moment and then she said, "Okay."

"What?"

"Nothing. I'm just getting tired. I should probably get to bed so I can get to work tomorrow. I just wanted to tell you what happened so you knew."

"It's a good thing you did," Samantha said. "Now we both

know Heather is someone who needs to be stopped."

"Yeah. I'll talk to you more tomorrow."

"Hey, before you go," Samantha said quickly. "I want to apologize for snapping at you the other day."

"Oh. It's okay."

"No, it's not. Especially that comment I made about you and Jeremy. It was unfair and mean. I shouldn't have said it. You guys are two different people than me and Steven and your relationship is different than ours too. Yours will progress at its own pace. I shouldn't have compared them."

"Sam, I understand. You're under a lot of stress with the wedding and your new job and now Heather. It's a lot. But the concerns I brought up over the weekend are still there. I get it that you want this wedding to be nice and what you dreamed it would be, but I just want you to keep in mind the reason you said yes to Steven's proposal in the first place."

Samantha let out a deep breath and started at the tiled floor. "I know. And I appreciate you saying something."

"Hey, we're sisters," Kathy said. "We keep each other in check."

"Yeah. Thank you."

"Of course. I just want you to remember that you should be focusing your energy on planning a happy marriage and not just a happy wedding. The day will come and go but Steven—and me—are still going to be there afterwards. So just keep that in mind."

CHAPTER 15

- OCTOBER 1976 -

The bed squeaked as Heather leaned over to pull on her boots. It was probably the worst part about the room. Dale always took her somewhere nicer than any other guy had before, but at the end of the day, all she really needed was a soft place to lay.

"That was fantastic," Dale gushed, still under the covers.

"So you had a good time then?"

He rubbed her back, but she stood to pull away from his touch. Boundaries were big with her. The deed was done, the money paid. If he wanted more, it would be an extra cost. No matter how nice he was, those were her rules.

"The best time," he said. "You are an amazing woman, Heather. I really appreciate our time together."

She smiled at him. "I'm glad."

"Can you please stay with me for the night?"

Heather chuckled. "Honey, you can't afford me for the full night."

There was no humor on Dale's face. "I'm serious. I want you to stay. I don't care how much it costs. You're special and we have a connection."

She had to agree. There was certainly chemistry between them that wasn't usually there with her other clients. But the fact of the matter was this arrangement was a no-strings-attached kind of deal. Embracing that connection blurred that line and, most important to her, cut into her wallet. Once a guy felt like he was her boyfriend, there came a sense of ownership, a give-and-take that strayed away from monetary payments and more into in-kind services like fancy dinners or plush hotel rooms.

Heather only wanted cash.

"You're a sweet guy," she said. "And I'm glad you've become a regular of mine. But I have other work to do. If you want me again, you know where to find me." She started to the door, but Dale called out to her.

"I think I'm falling in love with you."

Heather stopped and closed her eyes, letting out a heavy sigh. She saw the warning signs, knew he was getting kind of clingy, but she fed into that to squeeze more money out of his wallet. Now she was the one who had to pay.

Turning back to him, she kept her face completely expressionless. "If that's really how you feel, then we can't do this anymore."

"That's what I was thinking too!" He pulled back the covers and got to his feet. "I'm going to leave my wife. You can move in with me, stop risking your life on that corner every night." He stepped toward her.

She put up her hands and took a step backward to keep him at bay. "As much as I'd love to be off the street, that's not reality. What we do is a business transaction."

"But I love you."

"And those are the exact same words I'm sure you've said to your wife," she said. "And now you're just going to leave her because some other woman starts giving you attention?"

"It's not like that," he said. "My wife, she's—we got married so young! Now I know what love really is!"

"I don't think your wife appreciates you stepping out on her," Heather persisted.

"She doesn't know!"

She scoffed. "Women *always* know what their husbands are doing. Trust me, you're not that sneaky."

"But I want to be with you." His voice was small, realizing that he was fighting a losing battle.

"You know where I work and you know my rates," she told him. "Come find me then."

Heather turned and started for the door, but Dale called

out one more time.

"I promise you, I'll leave her."

With one hand on the doorknob, she gave him a sad smile as she shook her head. "That's not going to happen."

CHAPTER 16

*S*teven!" *Samantha called from her seat at the restaurant. She could see him walking toward Heather at the end of the pier.*

Samantha tried to get up, but something was holding her in her chair, trapping her.

"Steven!" she cried out again. Suddenly, the restaurant was empty. No one to hear her screams and help her out of her chair. No one to help stop her fiancé from being lured into Heather's trap.

From the end of the pier, Samantha could see Heather sneer at her as Steven approached her.

Finally, Samantha broke free from her invisible restraints and ran to catch up to him. Her heart raced and her legs pumped with all of its form, but the concrete pier suddenly took on a malleable consistency. Like running on the beach. Her feet swished out beneath her with each step, taking her longer to close the distance between her and Steven.

"Don't look at her!" she called to him, knowing it was no use. But it was better than staying silent. She needed to do something—anything—to prevent what she knew was coming.

Slowly, she was making headway. Each footstep brought her a smidge closer. Not close enough, but it was the best she could do.

Meanwhile, Heather sang. Words Samantha couldn't quite make out—maybe it was an ancient dialect or something—but the song was definitely audible. Magical. Casting a spell over Steven as he stopped directly in front of Heather.

"No!" Samantha shouted, but neither of them looked at her.

She felt like she was sinking now. Deeper into the concrete as if it were quicksand, but still she didn't stop. She kept plowing through as best she could, even as the waves from the lake filled the hole by her feet, slowly rising as she plunged through.

Heather ran the back of her hand along Steven's cheek and he leaned into it. She grazed his arm with her fingers, grasping his hand and hooking her free one around his waist.

"Stay away from him!" Samantha pleaded to Heather. Her feet had stopped moving, locked in by the water and quicksand. Her arms reached out along the concrete at her neck, pawing at the rough surface, trying desperately to get to him. Her fingers bled, but she didn't care. She needed to save him.

Heather leaned in to Steven and tilted her head with a smirk as he moved in to kiss her, resting his lips on her neck instead. She giggled, which sent rage through Samantha. But there was nothing the witch could do.

Samantha sunk deeper into the ground, but still she kept her eyes on the pair as best she could. Her strength was fading, but she refused to stop fighting.

Finally, Heather allowed him to press his lips to hers and fire consumed him, just as Samantha sank completely into the ground.

CHAPTER 17

Samantha lurched forward in bed, sweaty and breathless. She was disoriented and struggled to get her bearings as her eyes adjusted. The early morning light shone through the windows behind the sheer curtains, signifying the start of a new day. The tangle of sheets surrounded her, but most of the bedspread was on the floor.

Steven grunted beside her and reached out, but felt the puddle of sweat where she had been laying. He opened his eyes and saw her sitting upright. "What are you doing? Are you okay?"

She wiped the sweat from her forward and nodded. "Yeah, I'm fine. I just had a bad dream. Go back to sleep. You still have some time before the alarm will go off."

He closed his eyes and murmured, "Hmpf."

Slowly, she untangled herself from the sheets and stepped out of the room, just as she had done several hours earlier when Kathy called. She could feel her lack of sleep throughout her body as she stepped to the bathroom to freshen up.

In the mirror she saw a haggard woman staring back at her with dark circles under her eyes. Guess it would be a heavy make-up day today. Luckily her office had air conditioning. Maybe her weird dream was only the heat? She doubted it, especially as she recalled her conversation with Kathy in the middle of the night.

When she emerged from the bathroom, she had every intention of sneaking into Kathy's room to look in the magic book to figure out just what Heather was. Maybe if she had some concrete answers she would feel better and wouldn't be having such strange dreams. She doubted it, but maybe. Clarity always did have a way of making her feel better.

As she crossed the landing toward Kathy's room, a floorboard creaked and she cringed when she heard Steven call to her from the bedroom.

"Samantha? What are you doing?" A moment later, he opened her door and stood there in his underwear, his last defense to keeping cool in the night. He reached on the rack hanging on the back of her bedroom door for his bathrobe.

"I, uh, thought I heard something out front," she lied. "I was going to look through Kathy's window because I thought you would still be sleeping."

He pulled on his bathrobe and stepped toward her to wrap her in a hug. Despite the heat and sweat coming off his body, she leaned into it.

"I thought I might as well just get up now," he told her. "The sun's up and I was getting hot laying there."

She squirmed away from him. "Yeah, you're all sweaty."

He laughed and pulled her closer. "What? You don't like that?"

She giggled and pushed him away. "No! Get away from me."

Steven kissed the top of her head and then let her go. "I'm going to go down and make coffee. Do you want some?"

Samantha looked at the clock on the wall and sighed. "I should probably get in the shower. I can't stand feeling sticky this early in the morning."

"Can I join?"

She rolled her eyes. "What about your coffee?"

"I think I could find time for both."

Samantha laughed. "Oh yeah?"

"We never usually have the house to ourselves," he said. "Let's make the most of it."

As he pulled her in for another sweaty embrace, Samantha thought to herself that Heather could wait just a little bit longer. Steven was here and they were alone. Nothing bad was going to happen to him.

CHAPTER 18

The sun beaming in Kathy's eyes stirred her. She hadn't slept well at all. Between going to bed late, worrying about Paul and Heather, and what kind of threat she may be, she ended up tossing and turning all night. Not to mention the usual reasons she hadn't been sleeping lately.

She rolled over on Jeremy's bed and nearly crashed on the floor. Two adults in a full-size mattress didn't leave a lot of room for tossing and turning. But she managed to steady herself and reached for her watch beside the bed.

9:25

She jumped up to her feet. She was supposed to start work at 10:00, an hour before the restaurant opened. The opening shift helped wipe down tables, mop the floor, and get the kitchen in order for the day's rush. She figured she could be a little late for that, but it still took twenty minutes to drive there from Jeremy's house.

After combing her fingers out of her face and deciding that she could probably skip washing her hair for one day, she leaned over and shook her boyfriend gently.

"Jeremy, wake up," she said softly. "I need you to drive me to work."

He grunted and rolled over, pulling the blankets over his head. The heat apparently didn't bother him.

Kathy sighed and decided that she could get herself ready to go in order to give him some time to sleep in a little longer. She moved around his room and gathered her uniform from yesterday, fanning it out and deciding that the wrinkles weren't too bad for her to wear another day.

On her way out the door, she tapped Jeremy's foot. "I'm going to take a quick shower. I want to leave in twenty minutes. No later."

The rest of the house was quiet as she walked to the bathroom. Michael and Maddie were probably still sleeping, so she couldn't ask them for a ride either. As she stripped off her clothes and got in the shower—careful to pull her hair up to prevent it from getting wet and taking even longer to get ready—Kathy thought about her other options.

She could borrow Jeremy's car and drive herself, but that would mean he'd be without a car for the duration of the day and she didn't want to listen to *that* argument when he woke up and discovered she'd took it. Besides, with being around fryers all day, it would be almost impossible for her to get the stink of grease out of his car.

There was the bus, too, which she frequented often. But there was no direct line from Lawrence Park to Presque Isle and she had never taken that route before, so she didn't even know what the bus schedule was. Time was not on her side and she figured if she tried to take a bus and hop on different connections, it would probably take her a lot longer to get to work. Not to mention the fact that she'd have to walk down Peninsula Drive, the overbuilt highway leading into the park that was certainly not pedestrian friendly.

If Jeremy didn't wake up and get a move on, she'd have to call in. Not that she would mourn a day at a job she didn't like, but she was hourly. If she didn't work, she didn't get paid.

Turning off the water, she dried off and quickly got dressed, feeling her body already begin to sweat from the day's heat.

She opened the bathroom door and steam billowed out with her. Back in Jeremy's room, he hadn't moved. Except maybe his bottom lip drooping to let the drool drip onto the mattress.

Kathy shook his shoulder again, this time harder. "Jeremy, come on. I need you to take me to work."

He swatted her away and pulled the blanket tighter around himself. A move that told her he had no intention of getting up because she knew for a fact that he was probably overheating under it.

"If you don't get up, I'm going to have to call in," she pleaded.

"Then call in!"

Kathy stared down at him with her hands on her hips. A part of her was furious that he would be so selfish, but another part of her realized she shouldn't be surprised. Unless there was some sort of personal gain, Jeremy didn't help people. Even if he was sleeping with them.

Annoyed, she stormed out of the room and slammed his bedroom door. She wanted to piss him off, but once she got on the other side and heard the door echo throughout the quiet house, she regretted disturbing Michael and Maddie upstairs.

She went to the kitchen and dialed the restaurant.

"Sara's Diner, how can I help you?"

"Morrie, hi," Kathy started. "It's me. Look, I don't think I'm going to be able to get a ride in today."

There was a brief pause and then Morrie said, "Your shift starts in ten minutes."

"I know," she said. "I thought I'd have a ride but that fell through."

He sighed. "Well, Leah said she'd be running late. She usually goes right by your street. I could call her and see if she left—"

"I'm not home," Kathy said. "I'm at my boyfriend's."

Another sigh. "Okay. Well, since this is so close to the start of your shift, you're going to get a point for this. You know the rules, three points and it's an automatic fire. Doesn't matter how good of a worker you are when you're here. We need someone reliable."

"I know," she said. "And I'm sorry. I'll try to arrange for a better ride next time."

"You should get a car."

Kathy bit her bottom lip to keep in her sarcastic comment. As if buying a car and paying for it was so easy. Working as a checkout girl at a diner was not going to get her that kind of luxury. "I'll work on it, Morr."

She hung up and made pot of coffee. Now that it was going on ten o'clock, she figured the rest of the house would be getting up soon. Hopefully not Jeremy, though. She was still mad at him for making her call in that she didn't want to talk to him. Even if she and Samantha established that Steven and Jeremy needed to be protected from Heather.

Taking a seat on the couch with a cup of coffee, she stared out the window as the sun shone through the trees in the park across the street. There was already a couple kids outside playing, kicking a soccer ball back and forth.

She heard floors creak above her and then the sound of the stairs shifting. Too heavy to be Maddie and Jeremy's bedroom was downstairs. Must be Michael.

"Morning, Kathy," his voice confirmed it when he saw her

sitting on the couch. He had on a loose pair of shorts and a tank top.

"Morning," she replied. "I made coffee if you want some."

"Thanks." He poured himself a cup and then joined her on the couch.

"Did I wake you?" she asked. "I was mad at Jeremy, so I slammed the door. I'm sorry if it woke you up."

He shook his head after taking a sip. "Don't worry about it. I shouldn't be sleeping in this late anyway. I have things to do."

"How'd you sleep?" she asked. The implication behind her words registering with both of them.

Michael breathed in a deep breath and let it out slowly before responding. "Not good. My mind kept going with all kinds of different scenarios and conspiracy theories, you know?"

She nodded. "I've been thinking about it all night too."

"It's just…*weird*. The way it happened. I mean, we walked into the diner perfectly healthy and happy with our whole lives ahead of us and then…"

Kathy looked down at her cup of coffee to spare him the embarrassment of having an audience for his tears.

He quickly wiped at his eyes and then stared out the window to the soccer ball bouncing back and forth across the street. "That woman was a part of it, though. Somehow. She was humming or singing or something. It knocked all sense out of me."

Kathy looked up at him. "What do you mean?"

"Well, you saw me," Michael said. "I was ogling that woman—the one who was sitting by herself? I'm not one to have a wandering eye, but yesterday something just came over me. And Paul too, I'm assuming. He's never usually like that. Or rather, he *wasn't*."

"You mean, you didn't realize you were staring?"

"No, I knew," he said. "I just…couldn't look away. I don't know. It sounds dumb. Like an excuse, I guess."

"Walk me through it a bit."

Michael sighed and paused as he thought of a good explanation. "Well, I remember you and the other girls picking on me and Paul for staring, but it was like your voices were a distant echo. The whole thing was like I was looking down at myself with no control. Honestly, if Maddie hadn't been blocking me in, I probably would've approach the woman myself and done something I would've regretted. Or worse, maybe I would've ended up like Paul."

Kathy nodded and didn't say anything further. Inside, her mind was wandering with her own scenarios and conspiracy theories. There were too many oddities linked between men and Heather. And she needed to be stopped.

CHAPTER 19

Here are the files you wanted me to review." Samantha passed Mr. Marsden a stack of papers at his desk in the corner. Since it was still a growing accounting firm, the office space was small. They shared an open office space with cubicle walls for client privacy. However, Samantha could vouch for the fact that the fake walls were certainly not sound-proof.

"Wow, that was fast," Marsden said with a laugh. He took the papers from her and set them on his desk. "Do you have it in you to take another stack off my desk?"

Samantha eyed his desk, which had several coffee mugs—one of which had to have been from today—and powdered sugar from the donut he had with him when he came in this morning. No wonder his chair groaned every time he sat.

Among the sweets on his desk were stacks of papers that didn't seem to make any sense to Samantha, but she was sure Marsden knew exactly what everything was. Samantha liked to keep her own desk tidier than that, just so she could keep everything straight.

She even overhauled the firm's whole filing system for better access. But everyone had their own individual methods at their desks. And Samantha was still new, so she didn't want to leave a bad impression with any of her coworkers, least of all her boss.

"I was actually going to head out to lunch," she told him. "But I can start on a new stack this afternoon."

"That would be fantastic." He waved his hands over the stacks of papers and seemed to grab one at random. "Here, take this. Hopefully after this week we can get through all of this audit nonsense and be rid of the IRS for a little bit. Ha!"

She smirked. "I'll start on this right after lunch."

"Take your time," he said, reaching for his own bagged lunch behind his desk. "I know you're good for it."

Samantha returned to her cubicle, dropped off the stack of papers, and then went down to the break room at the end of the hall. Despite Steven's temptations that morning, she had managed to pack both of them a lunch. Already practicing her wifely duties. Not that she had planned to fully adhere to the stereotypical "wife" mold once she officially was one.

She retrieved her lunch from the break room refrigerator and returned to her cubicle. Ordinarily, she would either eat in the break room—a good way to get to know her coworkers—or go for a walk. Today, she wanted to check in on Steven. She knew she was just being paranoid, but with the threat of Heather on the loose—and the fact that she hadn't had a chance to identify exactly what she was—Samantha wanted to be sure he was all right.

"This is Steven Harper, how can I help you?"

"Steven, hi, it's Samantha."

"Oh, hi! To what do I owe the pleasure?"

"I'm on my lunch and I just thought we could talk." She propped the phone against her ear and opened her container with her salad. She dribbled Italian dressing over top.

"I'm glad you called," he said. "I wanted to talk to you about something."

"Yeah?" She stabbed the lettuce leaves with her fork.

"My mom called me today to ask if there was anything she could do to help with the wedding planning."

Samantha's stomach dropped. Despite being together for three years, they hadn't really interacted with each other's parents much. Well, Steven wouldn't ever meet Samantha's parents.

"She was kind of upset when I told her that we already started," he went on. "And she pointed out that they hadn't really met you. I didn't even realize that."

"Hmm," Samantha murmured. So far in their relationship, it had always worked out that there was some reason every holiday and get-together that Samantha couldn't join his family, which meant they had avoided officially meeting. Now, the ring on Samantha's left hand threw out all excuses not to.

"She wants us to come over for dinner tonight," he said.

"Tonight?" Samantha nearly started choking when she blurted it out.

"Yeah, we don't have anything going on, do we?"

Her mind raced as she tried to come up with a plausible reason not to. There were several reasons—like, for instance, why hadn't his mother ever made an effort to meet her before they were engaged?—but she couldn't bring that up to Steven.

First of all, she was worried that Steven's parents wouldn't like her. Any parent would be standoffish to their son's fiancée, especially one who they hadn't met until after they had already started planning the wedding.

And second, she wanted to get home to identify what type of creature Heather was and touch base with Kathy again so they could figure out a way to stop her and save Steven and Jeremy.

But if Samantha was going to keep Steven safe, she needed to keep an eye on him. What better way to do that then to go to dinner? She and Kathy could brainstorm a strategy when she got home.

Besides, she would need to meet Steven's parents sooner or later. Better get it done before anything was official.

"No, we don't have anything," she finally responded.

Siren

"What's the matter?"

"I'm just nervous."

"Don't be," he said. "They'll love you."

Easy for you to say, she thought.

"So meet you at your house after work?" she asked.

"Yeah, I'll drive us out there. They don't live too far away. Just on the edge of the city."

"Okay then. I guess I'm meeting the parents today."

CHAPTER 20

Kathy unlocked the front door and stepped into her empty house with Jeremy in tow. She was grateful to get out of the hot, stuffy car. Even though they had the windows rolled down, the passing air did nothing to relieve the tension between them after their argument that morning. The heat only added to their anger.

Jeremy went straight to the couch and plopped down. Kathy walked around and opened the windows.

"Let's get some air moving in here," she murmured, partly to herself and partly in the hopes that it would break the silence between her and Jeremy.

In response, he grabbed the remote control and turned on the TV.

Kathy sighed audibly, but moved on to the next room's windows. She debated saying something to him, about how he had no right to be mad at her for waking him up because he told her he'd take her to work in the morning, but she ultimately decided against it.

Paul just died, completely unexpected. And murdered, for that matter. Jeremy was going through a lot right now and if this was how he worked through those emotions, Kathy needed to support him. Besides, he did agree to come home with her. Reluctantly.

With the windows open and a slight breeze drifting through the house, Kathy started up the stairs to get the magic book. Samantha had called her at lunch and told her she hadn't had a chance to ID Heather in the magic book so now it was up to Kathy.

She stopped halfway up the stairs and looked back at Jeremy. He stared blankly at the TV, his feet sprawled out on the antique coffee table and his neck propped up by the cushions on the back of the couch. She wished there was more she could do for him—she debated putting off looking in the book and laying with him, but even if he was comforted for the moment, she wouldn't be doing him any favors if Heather got the better of him and he wound up dead.

Just like Paul.

With that, she continued up the stairs and went to her bedroom. She didn't close the door completely, but left a gap open in case Jeremy called for her. The last thing she needed was to be interrupted while looking through her family's magical tome.

Kneeling beside the bed, she pulled out *The Art of Magic* from underneath. It was a large, leather-bound book containing all of the knowledge her family had gained about magical beings through the years. It didn't always contain the answers she and her sister sought, but it was certainly helpful in more cases than not.

She flipped open the cover, listening to the satisfying crackle of the spine. Turning the pages, she went to the section titled, "Species" and flipped through, scanning each of the pages, looking for anything that resembled what she knew about Heather.

Banshee? No, Heather used a song to lure men, not a scream to kill them. Besides, Banshees weren't particular about men. They went after anyone they targeted.

Possibly an Enchantress, which was a witch that specialized in magic related to love. Heather seemed to be going after couples, but that didn't explain the way that Paul died. If a witch specialized in love, they didn't also have a firepower.

She kept looking.

Finally, she found the entry on Sirens and read it to herself.

Sirens are women whose enchanting songs make them irresistible to men. The lure of their music draws committed men in loving relationships to betray their love, resulting in their fiery demise.

While men in loving relationships are the targets and are susceptible to the lure of the Siren's song, women are able to hear the song as well, and are drawn by it to witness their partner's betrayal.

It is believed that the only way to defeat a Siren is to overpower the strength of her song with a voice even more beautiful than her own, however, there is a theory that binding a Siren's hands in rope would also limit her power.

Hmm, Kathy thought to herself. *No official way to kill her, only weaken her.*

The information wasn't completely useless. At least now she understood what Heather was and what she wanted. But unless they used Steven and Jeremy as bait, there was no way to be sure where she was and when she would make her move. They needed to be prepared for anything.

Kathy stashed the book back under her bed and went downstairs. She didn't want to be too far away from Jeremy for too long, even if they were annoyed with each other at the moment.

"Hey, get me something to eat," he called to her as she came down the stairs. He couldn't even take his eyes off the TV.

She stared at him, her hands on her hips, waiting for him to rephrase the question or add a simple, "Please."

Nothing.

"Kath?" He raised his eyebrows, but his eyes were still locked on the TV.

"Seriously? You can't get it yourself?"

"What?" he asked, finally looking at her now.

"That was rude," she said. *Just like you blowing me off this morning*, she thought, but didn't voice it.

"You're the one that dragged me here," he countered. "And then you ignore me the whole ride over and run upstairs as soon as we get here. What, am I just a ride to you?"

"No, of course not," she said. "I just—"

"You can't be bothered by the fact that one of my best friends just died. It's too inconvenient for you."

Kathy huffed because she didn't want to say the first thing that came to her mind: that he hadn't ever talked about Paul until he asked to move in. Jeremy even complained about it to Kathy, saying that Paul was annoying. Now that he was dead he was suddenly Jeremy's best friend?

That thought was followed closely by her next one: how heartless could she be for getting mad at Jeremy for grieving in his own way? It had been less than twenty-four hours and she had already isolated him from Michael and Maddie.

But it was for his own good, she told herself. What if Heather went after Jeremy when she wasn't around? Would she hear the Siren's song even if she wasn't nearby?

"You forced me to come here and now you're picking a fight," he said.

"I'm sorry," Kathy said. "I just thought you could use some comfort."

"And this is your idea of comfort?" He sat up, now fully agitated. "Newsflash: yelling is not comforting!"

She stared at him, not sure what to say. Not sure if anything she said would change the way he felt. She knew part of this was his frustration with the fact that Paul was dead. He was just taking it out on her. But he did have a point. She was being insensitive because she couldn't tell him the truth about why she needed him to come home with her.

Finally, Jeremy got to his feet and grabbed his keys from the table. "Never mind. I should've just dropped you off. I'm going home."

"No!" Kathy called, reflexively.

Jeremy didn't stop.

She put up her hands and froze him in place with his hand on the doorknob, about to open it.

Taking a deep breath to calm herself, Kathy stepped toward her boyfriend, frozen in time by her magic. For the first time, she saw the pain on his face, hidden behind a mask of anger. She saw her role in the way he felt, the way he was acting. It was always something between them.

"Why does everything have to be so hard for us?" she asked, not expecting a response. This was something she needed to say to him, but had never had the courage to say it to his face.

"I feel like we're constantly treading water, just barely keeping afloat enough to breathe before a wave comes by and chokes us." She looked up at the ceiling, blinking away frustrated tears. "I look at Samantha and Steven and everything is so easy with them. They fit and work together and respect each other. I wish that could be us. Maybe it will someday, but right now I'm just…unhappy."

She debated telling him all of this to his face once she unfroze him, but decided against it. That would be like rubbing salt in his wounds. They needed space before she could bring this up. Too bad space was something they wouldn't have the luxury of enjoying with the threat of Heather looming over them.

Kathy took a step back and unfroze him, quickly reaching for his arm. "Jeremy, wait."

He turned. His jaw clenched and his eyes darting around the room, refusing to look at her. Refusing to allow her to see what was clearly laid out on his face.

"I want you to stay," she said. "I don't think being at your apartment will be good for you right now. There are too many memories of Paul. And I'm sorry for yelling. You're going through a lot and I didn't see that."

He swallowed and nodded, but didn't say anything else.

"Do you want to talk about it?"

"No."

"Do you want to just lay on the couch for a while?" she asked.

He nodded and she led him back to the living room, carefully taking his keys from him and setting them back on the table. They collapsed on the couch together, with Kathy latched on his arm and Jeremy staring at the TV, a shell of himself.

It wasn't perfect. None of their problems had been resolved. They still didn't completely work. But for now, it was enough.

CHAPTER 21

Samantha's heart wouldn't stop racing all day the closer it got to quitting time. By time she pulled in front of Steven's house and put the car in park, her hands were shaking too.

She tried to ignore her anxiety about meeting his parents as she gathered her purse, checked her makeup in the mirror, and got out of the car to knock on Steven's door. She was just nervous about meeting new people—people she would soon become family with.

Steven answered the door shortly after Samantha knocked. She could've went in—like she usually did—but she didn't want to linger. She wanted to get this dinner over with as quickly as possible.

"Hey," he said with a smile when he opened the door. He

leaned forward and kissed her before reaching back and closing the door behind him. "Ready to go?" Despite the heat, he was wearing jeans and a white button-down shirt that he tucked in. A more casual look than Samantha's business attire, having just come from the office.

She tried to swallow down her nerves. "Um, yeah. I guess so."

"Don't worry," he said over his shoulder as he locked the door. "They'll love you."

"You keep saying that." She followed him down the porch steps to the driveway where his car was parked on the end.

He opened the driver door and cranked the window down. "Let's give it a second to cool off before we head out. The sun's been brutal today."

Samantha nodded and stood on the sidewalk, trying to figure out what to do with her hands. Stuffing them in her pockets proved too hot, resting them on the strap of her purse only tugged at her neck and she didn't need more tension there. She settled for clasping them in front of her.

"What's the matter?" Steven asked. "You're quiet. That's not like you."

She smiled at his joke. "Well, since you kind of sprung this dinner on me last-minute—"

"I told you at lunch!"

Samantha shot him a look. "That would be last-minute, sweetie."

He put up his hands in surrender.

"Anyway, since I didn't have significant warning of this dinner, I think there needs to be a trade-off." She'd been plotting this ultimatum of sorts since she got off the phone with him at lunch.

"A trade-off?" Steven asked. "Samantha, I'm asking you to meet my parents, not drink poison."

Same difference, Samantha thought, but didn't voice it.

"If I go to your parents' for dinner, I think it's only fair that you come back home with me and spend the night."

He grinned and stepped toward her, putting his hands on her hips and leaning in. "Oh? Couldn't get enough last night?" He kissed her cheek.

She smiled and stepped back, immediately thinking about her dream last night and Heather. "Something like that. We're going to be married, so that means that we need to adjust to living together. I don't want any surprises to come up after we say 'I do' and have us second-guessing our decision."

"You think living together is going to make me second-guess marrying you?" he asked.

She shrugged. "Better to find out while we each still have a place to go that's away from each other. Just don't pee on the toilet seat and everything should go fine."

He laughed. "Okay. I think I can manage that."

"Good. Now let's go meet your parents."

Steven didn't move to the car..

"Is there something else?" Samantha asked on her way to her side of the car.

"Um…" He reached up and scratched his forehead. "No, never mind. It's not important."

"Are you sure?"

"Yeah, let's go," he said, moving to the car. "We don't want to be late."

CHAPTER 22

Steven's parents lived in a makeshift cul-de-sac on the edge of the city limits. One street over and they'd technically be in Millcreek Township. Their ranch-style house looked similar to all the others around, with the garage extending out into the driveway, keeping the front door hidden from view.

Samantha always felt like these houses sent the message: "Go away, we don't want you here." But then, she had grown up in an old house where the front door was prominent. Not to mention, at the moment, she didn't want to be a part of this dinner and that was altering her impression of the house.

"The gardens look nice," Samantha said to Steven as they walked up. It was her way of making up for her initial negative thoughts.

"Oh yeah, my mom spends a fortune on them," Steven said. "Tell her how much you like them and that'll get you brownie points."

"Do I need brownie points?" she asked.

He shrugged. "It wouldn't hurt."

That didn't help Samantha feel any better.

Steven knocked on the front door and then stepped in. "Mom? Dad? I'm here with Samantha."

They walked into an entryway with linoleum flooring and a cased-opening to the dining room just to their right. In the center of the house was a large room with white tile covered by a beige shag area rug and living room furniture pointed toward a large entertainment center. The walls were white with few decorations. To Samantha, this house felt cold and empty compared to her own house.

Around the other side of the dining room, a shrill woman's voice echoed throughout the cavernous house. "Steven! My sweet boy!"

Samantha followed Steven in as he hugged his mother. She was a small, plump woman whose short blonde hair was styled to almost stand up on end, with the exception of the large bangs. Samantha could smell the hairspray wafting off of her with every movement.

"Mom, I'd like you to meet my fiancée, Samantha Walker," Steven said, extending his arm out to Samantha.

She stepped forward, hoping Steven would hook his arm

around her to help give her something to do. Instead, he nearly pushed her toward his mother, who extended a limp hand.

"Well, it's about time you came around here," she said with a fake smile. "I was afraid you were going to snatch my boy away and we'd never see him again."

Samantha tried to retain her poise. "Oh, no. Steven's his own person."

"Of course he is!" his mother said, then turned to her son. "Now, Grandpa Jack decided to stop over. I told him we had company coming, but you know how he likes to just drop in."

"That's okay," Steven said. "He can meet Samantha then too."

Samantha remained silent. She didn't feel comfortable with this family reunion. She felt like a fly on the wall in a place she wasn't supposed to be.

"Could you be a dear and make sure he's not sitting in the sun?" Mrs. Harper asked him. "He really shouldn't be out there too long with the medication he's on."

"Where's Dad?" he asked.

"Oh, in the garage," she said. "He just finished watering my flowers."

"I think your gardens are beautiful," Samantha added quickly.

Mrs. Harper stared at her with a bright smile that was once again obviously forced. "Thank you, dear. I'd certainly hope so for as much as I paid for them."

Steven cleared his throat. "I'll go check on Grandpa. Why don't you two get to know each other?"

Samantha watched him exit out the sliding glass door off the kitchen and tried to telepathically plead with him not to leave her alone with his mother, but he left her stranded regardless.

Mrs. Harper turned her attention back to the kitchen and fussed. Samantha could tell she was trying everything in her power to not talk to her.

"So is this the house that Steven grew up in?" Samantha asked.

Mrs. Harper pulled the lid off the pot on the stove, delicious aromas filling the air. She shook her head with her back to Samantha. "No, dear. His father and I moved here after he started college."

"Oh. Well, it's a beautiful house," she said, hoping to gain more brownie points with her future mother-in-law after the compliment on her garden fell flat.

"Thank you."

Once again, Samantha was stuck with nothing to do and nothing to say. Just standing there as if she were invisible.

The door to the right of the kitchen swung open and a man stepped out. His stained white T-shirt was pulled tight over his large belly.

"Martin, do you mind?" Mrs. Harper sneered at him. "We have a guest."

"Oh, I'm sorry." He wiped his hand on his jeans and then extended it to Samantha. "You must be Steven's girl. I'm his dad."

She smiled at him. "Nice to meet you."

"Steven didn't do this girl justice!" he said to his wife. He turned back to Samantha. "You're beautiful!"

"Yes, yes, she's very pretty," Mrs. Harper said. "Would you mind getting cleaned up so we can eat? This is almost ready."

"Aye, aye, madam!" He looked at Samantha. "Excuse me a moment."

Steven came back inside. "Grandpa's getting hungry."

"Tell him to put a sock in it," Mrs. Harper said. "It's almost done."

"So, what have you two been talking about?" Steven asked.

"Don't be nosy, darling," Mrs. Harper said.

"I met your dad," Samantha offered.

"And what'd you think?"

Samantha looked over at Steven's mother's back and then to him. Why would he put her on the spot like that? He probably didn't even realize it, but still. "He seems nice."

"He's been working in the yard all day," Mrs. Harper said, turning back to them. "He's a total mess. You'll see, he'll clean up better once he's had a shower, which hopefully won't take him too long."

"Is there anything I can do to help with dinner?" Samantha asked.

Siren

"That's very kind of you, dear, but I have it under control," Mrs. Harper said quickly. "Why don't you go out and get to know Grandpa Jack? Keep him company until dinner's ready."

"Uh, okay." Samantha gave a pleading look to Steven, who didn't seem to notice just how badly she was drowning with his mother. She stepped through the sliding doors onto the concrete patio where Grandpa Jack was seated at a glass outdoor table with an umbrella raised through the middle.

"Hi," she said in a small voice and extended her hand. "I'm Steven's girlfriend—fiancée—Samantha."

Jack gripped her hand hard with his small, rough hand, and nodded. "Nice to meet you. Have a seat."

She took a seat beside him, against the house, and looked out across the yard. The house sat up on a small hill and they could see several streets over. If downtown Erie had skyscrapers, Samantha guessed that they'd be able to see them from here.

The fresh air and comfortable silence with Jack gave her some reprieve from the tension growing inside. Then again, she knew exactly why Mrs. Harper suggested she go out and sit with Grandpa. She wanted to talk to Steven about who he brought home.

Samantha tried not to think about that as she waited. Instead, she focused on the setting sun and the beautiful landscaping. The gardens from the front extended out back as well.

Finally, Steven, Mrs. Harper, and Mr. Harper all emerged from inside, carrying paper plates, salad, and a steaming dish of pasta. Mr. Harper took drink orders from everyone and ran in and out of the house bringing out cups.

Once everyone was seated, they all dished out their meals in silence until Mr. Harper spoke up.

"So Samantha, you live in Erie?"

She nodded and wiped her mouth in a napkin before she spoke. "Mm-hmm. Over on Arlington."

"That's a nice part of town," he said. "We used to live over by Gridley Park, which was nice, but the neighborhood's changing." He raised his hand and shook it. "A lot of sketchy people moving in to those houses."

"Luckily, we got this house," Mrs. Harper gushed. "It's such a quiet street and we're the first owners of this house. No more spending loads of money on fixing the mistakes of previous owners."

"Do you have those kind of problems with your house?" he asked.

"Some, but not too bad,"she responded.

"You own a house?" Mrs. Harper asked with her eyebrows raised, clearly impressed.

Samantha nodded. "Me and my sister, yeah. It's been in our family for a long time. Probably a hundred years."

"What about your parents?" she asked.

"Mom," Steven said as a warning.

"What? It's not like we're never going to meet them," she said. "I would assume they're coming to the wedding?"

"Mom!"

Samantha put her hand on Steven's arm—who thankfully decided to sit beside her—and said, "No, it's okay."

"Did I miss something?" Mr. Harper asked. He looked between his wife and son.

"Well, my mom died when I was younger," Samantha said. "And my father..." She breathed in a deep breath before continuing. "He, uh, went on what he called a 'soul-searching' trip that was only supposed to last a couple months. But that was back when I first started college and I just graduated in May and still have yet to see or hear from him, so..."

"Oh," Mrs. Harper said, clearly taken by surprise.

"Yeah."

"We didn't mean to bring it up," Mr. Harper said as an apology for his wife.

"How'd you pay for college?" Grandpa Jack asked.

"Dad," Mr. Harper said.

Samantha shrugged. "I had to work while going to school. Kathy helped, my sister. Of course, it also meant that *she* couldn't go to college." She waved it off. "But now that I've graduated and it's all paid off, I can help Kathy pay for college if she wants, just as soon as we get a handle on the bills that we got a bit behind on."

The table was quiet, but Samantha still felt like everyone

was looking at her even though all eyes were everywhere *but* on her.

"For being early in the season, these cherry tomatoes are quite good," Mrs. Harper said as a way to change the subject. "Have you tried yours yet?"

Samantha kept her head down and finished eating. She felt Steven slide his hand on her leg and squeeze it. She hadn't ever told him the story of her parents, either. At least now he knew. And she knew that he was still there for her.

CHAPTER 23

I'm sorry for my parents tonight," Steven said once they pulled away from the Harpers' house.

"It's fine." Samantha sat with her arms crossed and looked out the window, away from Steven. She wasn't necessarily mad at him, she was just mad and he was the easiest target.

"If I would've realized they were going to—"

"Not they," she corrected. "Your *mother*. She was very cold to me."

He sighed. "Yeah, she can be like that sometimes. But it's only because she's protective of me because it's just me. They don't have any other kids."

"That was not protection," Samantha countered. She leaned as Steven turned onto Wayne Street back into the city. "She didn't even *try* to get to know me. She was marking her territory and making it clear that I wasn't welcome. And then at dinner, when I answered the question *your father* asked, I was completely ignored."

"I'm sorry," he said again. "I wish it had gone differently, but it didn't. Maybe if we didn't wait until we were engaged to introduce you—"

"I really don't think it would've mattered."

He huffed. "Okay." He put on his signal to turn left onto Pine Avenue and cursed under his breath as the traffic and the lights were not working in his favor to make the turn. Finally, after he was frustrated, he gunned the car and raced onto Pine, running a yellow light as he did.

"What, are you mad now too?"

"I'm not mad, Samantha," he said in a tone that suggested he was. "I'm just frustrated."

"How do you think I feel?" she asked, her voice growing loud.

"And what do you want me to do about it?" he shouted back, stopping at the red light at East 28th Street.

She sighed and said, "There's nothing you can do. It was just embarrassing to be so obviously judged for things out of my control. Yes, okay, I should've met them sooner than today, but I didn't. They need to get over that. We're all adults here and, not to toot my own horn, but it's not like you brought home some trash from the corner. I'm a good person and we have something real here." She wiped the wetness off her face.

Steven reached over and squeezed her hand just before letting it go to retake the steering wheel when the light turned green. He turned onto Parade Street. "Of course you're a good person. And I'm sorry you felt like you were judged. I'll talk to my mom—"

"You don't have to do that."

"Of course I do. She needs to know that what she said wasn't right and that you were upset by it. She's not going to change until people start calling her on it."

She looked over at him. "You're going to stand up to your mother?"

He glanced over at her, then returned his eyes to the road. "For you, I'd do anything."

Samantha patted his leg. "I love you."

"I love you too. I won't let this happen again."

"Thanks."

Steven didn't say anything until he stopped at the next red light. "So can we talk about the fact that that was the first time *I* heard the story of your parents? That's horrible, Sam."

She shrugged. "We got through it."

"Doesn't make it right."

"If I went through life thinking everything was fair, I would be incredibly disappointed," she said. "We got through it and now we're moving on. I still have Kathy. I didn't lose my whole family. And now I'm gaining you."

"And my family will come around."

"Sure."

"I would like you to do one thing for me, if you could," he started.

"What's that?"

"I think it would be a good idea if you tracked your dad down and invited him to the wedding."

She was already saying 'No' before he finished. "Steven, I have no idea where he is. And that's okay. I don't need to know. I've dealt with it and I've moved on. Abandoning us was a choice he made. Hunting him down and inviting him to the wedding is only going to open a can of words I've worked really hard to close. Besides, that would involve Kathy too and I'm not going to change her life for my wedding."

"I just think you'll feel differently when you see my family there, celebrating and you only have Kathy."

"Kathy's the only one I need," Samantha said. "She's the one who's been there. We help each other, we get through things together. *That's* what family is."

"Okay," he said with a sigh. "I just want you think about it. We still have time before the wedding."

"I'm not going to change my mind."

He nodded. "Okay. Then that's your choice."

A few minutes later, Steven pulled into his driveway and shut off the car, but didn't move to get out.

"Look, I know you said you wanted me to come over

tonight, but if you need space I'll just stay here. I get it. Tonight wasn't easy for you. But thank you for coming and suffering through it."

She gave him a half-smile. "Hey, we're going to be family soon. That's what family does."

Steven put his hand on the side of her face. "Absolutely."

She leaned in and kissed him. "I would like you to come home with me."

He sat back and raised his eyebrows. "Yeah?"

"Don't get too excited," she said. "I have no idea what Kathy's doing. I just think that making up before we go to bed angry is a skill we need to work on before we officially become husband and wife. I have a feeling you're going to be annoying me a lot once we're married." She smirked so he knew she was kidding.

"Sure, Sam. It's not at all because you want me."

She laughed and pushed him away, opening her door to step out. "Actually, I could do without sleeping next to the furnace in this sweltering heat."

He got out and met her behind his car and hugged her. "Am I too hot for you, baby?"

She laughed again and let him dip her so he could plant another kiss on her.

"Okay, get me back on my feet," she said with a smile. "I'm going home. I'll see you soon, okay?"

"Yes, ma'am!"

She stepped to her car and got in, still smiling to herself. As she pulled away, she couldn't help but feel lucky for having him in her life.

CHAPTER 24

Kathy heard Samantha and Steven come up the steps of the front porch before they entered. She and Jeremy had both nodded off in front of the TV. The room was dark, but still stuffy. They must've fallen asleep before the sun set.

Steven walked in first and did a double-take when he saw Kathy and Jeremy begin to sit up.

"What is it?" Samantha asked him before she came around the corner and saw them for herself. "Oh, you're home. Why are all the lights off?"

Kathy stretched before reaching over and flicking on the lamp beside the couch. "We fell asleep."

Jeremy leaned forward on his knees and rubbed his eyes. Groggily, he asked, "How you doing?"

Steven stuffed his hands in his pockets and gave them a tight smile. "I didn't think you guys would be home."

"Well, we stayed at Jeremy's last night, so…" Kathy trailed off. She could tell Steven wanted to have another uninterrupted night with Samantha.

"So what did you guys do today?" Samantha stepped around the room and turned on the other lamps. The downside of having an old house was that overhead lighting was not a thing when the house was built.

Kathy and Jeremy looked at each other and she shrugged. "Not much. It's…it's been a long day."

"A long two days," Jeremy clarified.

"Yeah, Kathy told me," Samantha said. "I'm sorry about your friend. How are you holding up?"

He looked at the floor and shook his head slightly. "I don't really want to talk about it."

Kathy rubbed his back.

"You know, I think I'm just going to go upstairs," he said. "I'm sorry."

"Don't be," Samantha said. "It's okay. We understand."

He stood and trotted up the stairs.

"What happened?" Steven asked.

Samantha and Kathy looked at each other before Samantha whispered to him, "His friend died…unexpectedly yesterday."

Steven looked toward the stairs where Jeremy had departed. "That's horrible."

"Yeah." Kathy gathered the sweatshirt Jeremy had left on the couch and hung it over the back. "It was sudden and kind of…unusual."

"Unusual?" Steven took a seat on the arm of a nearby chair and crossed his arms. "Was it just because he was young?"

"Well, yeah," Kathy said. "But there was more."

"I'll explain later," Samantha added.

Steven nodded and accepted the fact that the topic was over for now.

"How was dinner?" Kathy asked.

Samantha looked over at Steven. "The food was good."

"That bad?"

"Growing pains," Steven clarified.

"If you can call my total embarrassment growing pains," Samantha said.

"Hey, I said I'd talk to my mother," he said.

Kathy put up her hands. "Forget I asked!"

"We'll be fine," Samantha said. She turned to her fiancé. "There are some things we need to discuss a bit more."

"You guys'll figure it out," Kathy said. "You love each other. That's all you need."

Neither of them said anything for a while until Steven declared he was going up to bed too. After he was gone, Kathy turned off the TV and followed her sister into the kitchen, where she proceeded to put a kettle on the stove to make tea.

"Steven seemed a little annoyed that Jeremy and I were

here." Kathy lifted herself up onto the counter, leaning against the cabinets.

"It's been a long day." Samantha pulled down the box of tea bags from a cupboard. "Being engaged is harder than we thought."

"So his parents were kind of a nightmare?"

"His *mother* was kind of a nightmare," Samantha clarified. "And she was the one I was most nervous about."

"Well, you expected the worst and that's what you got. It can only go up from here, right?"

"Let's hope. She was just so dismissive of me. Like I was a horrible person. And then the topic of our parents came up—"

"Uh oh."

"Exactly. I was honest with them—it was even the first time I told Steven the whole story—but it obviously killed the mood after. Everyone was too afraid to ask me anything else about myself."

"I'm sure they were just shocked," Kathy offered. "Especially Steven. You really hadn't told him about Dad before?"

Samantha flicked through the tea options. "No. I guess I didn't want him to feel bad for me or anything. I didn't want him to be with me out of pity."

"At this point, I think it's obviously he's not with you out of pity," Kathy said. "He loves you. Who cares what his family thinks?"

"Easier said than done." Samantha pulled a mug out of the

cupboard. "You want some?"

"Sure."

Samantha pulled a second mug out and moved them beside the stove.

"Have you given any thought to revealing some of your other secrets to Steven?" Kathy asked.

"Other secrets?"

"You know, the one you and I both share."

Samantha breathed in a deep breath. "Oh. That one."

"If you two are going to be married—and I would assume he's going to move in—then it's going to get harder to hide certain things from him," Kathy said. "Besides, do you really want to keep secrets from your husband?"

"I've been doing it for three years so far, I've kind of gotten used to it."

"Is that a habit you want to continue?"

"I don't know, Kathy," she said. "I just don't want it to ruin anything. That's a big reveal."

"I know it is, but the longer you put it off, the harder it's going to be for him to wrap his head around."

"And what about you and Jeremy? Are you going to tell him?"

"Jeremy and I aren't as serious as you guys," Kathy said. "At least, we're nowhere near marriage." Yet another reminder that she wasn't living in Samantha's shadow. To live in her shadow would mean that she was close to achieving the same things as her sister. She wasn't.

The kettle whistled and Samantha pulled it off the stove. "Anyway, before we take a deep dive into overanalyzing our relationships, perhaps we should talk about the most pressing thing threatening them?" She filled the cups and slid one over to her sister.

Kathy reached for a tea bag and ripped the package open. "I'm assuming you're not referring to your future mother-in-law?"

"Funny, but no. What did you find out about Heather?" Samantha decided to keep the dreams she'd been having to herself. "And what exactly happened with Paul?"

Kathy knew her sister was looking for specifics. "Well, from the brief time I had to look at the book when Jeremy and I got home, my best guess is that Heather's a Siren," she explained. "Their songs draw men who are in loving relationships to them to betray their love and then the Siren kills them in a 'fiery demise' or something like that. According to the book, women can hear the same song as their men, but they're not drawn to it and hypnotized by it like men are."

"Which has been our experience," Samantha said. "Is that what happened with Paul?"

Kathy nodded. "I think so, yeah. His mouth was all scorched. It's like she had the kiss of death or something."

"Maybe it was *burning* passion."

Kathy shot her sister a look. "He was a good guy."

"You're right. I shouldn't be making jokes. I'm sorry," Samantha said. "Did the book list a way to stop her?"

"One way was to overpower the strength of her song with something that sounds even more beautiful than hers."

"Seeing how her song is probably magically amplified, that's going to be a hard one to pull off. What else was there?"

"Binding her hands in rope would limit her power," Kathy said.

Samantha rocked her head back and forth. "I suppose you could freeze her and then we could tie her hands."

"But unless I'm able to freeze her with her hands together, I'm not going to be able to move her to tie them together."

"Hmm." Samantha took a careful sip of her tea. "We'll have to think of something. Anyway to find her?"

Kathy shook her head. "Not that I could see. I thought about going to the library to look at some mythology books, but with Jeremy here I wasn't going to leave him. He would have no reason to stay here, and he's already not happy about the fact that I forced him out of his house. I can't exactly drag him to the library, either. He's grieving."

"Yeah," Samantha said. "We'll just have to keep an eye on them until she shows up again. At least we know what she wants."

"Men, particularly those who are committed," Kathy said.

Samantha raised her cup to her mouth. "Those usually are the best ones."

Kathy laughed. "Good thing you've already locked yours down." She indicated her sister's engagement ring.

"Not officially yet."

"It will be soon enough."

"Yeah, when we can plan this wedding." A thought struck her. "There was a woman on the boat when we first saw Heather when we were at the lighthouse with Cheryl and Steven."

Kathy squinted her eyes. "I don't remember. I was more focused on the fact that he was racing to the shore. Why?"

"Well, I'm just thinking, if Sirens push men to betray their love, I wonder if they also punish the ones who have already betrayed their relationships."

"You think he was stepping out on someone he loved?"

"Well, there were plenty of other guys on the beach she could've picked from that were not far from where she was standing," Samantha reasoned. "Hell, last weekend Presque Isle was swarming with people—families. Lots of married men for her to steal away. But how many of them were cheaters?"

"Probably more than I want to think about."

"Maybe none of them were brave enough to spend a day at the beach with their floozy?"

"Floozy?" Kathy laughed.

"You know what I mean."

"Okay, so you think she was targeting that guy on Saturday because he was actively out with someone who was not his love? Then why go after Steven and Jeremy? We both had run-ins with her with our guys. In my case, she even killed Paul." Kathy didn't want to voice the fact that Jeremy hadn't been called by Heather's song like Paul and Michael were.

"She went after them because they're how she can get to us," Samantha said. "We stopped her from getting her target on Saturday, so *we* became her targets."

"Except her magic doesn't work on women, so she went after Steven and Jeremy instead," Kathy finished. "So what does that mean for us?"

"It means that if we don't stop her, Steven and Jeremy will see the same fiery demise that Paul did."

CHAPTER 25

Kathy rolled over in bed, sweating. It was still dark and the clock on the side of her bed told her it was nearly two in the morning. The fan at the foot of the bed offered some relief from the heat, but it couldn't subdue the radiant heat coming from Jeremy on the other side of the bed.

She let out a heavy breath and stared at the ceiling. She debated whether she wanted to get up and use the bathroom and get a drink of water from the kitchen. It was a long walk to the kitchen, but she needed some relief from the heat.

Kathy brought her feet to the floor—which was refreshingly cool compared to her warm bedspread—and padded to the door, careful not to wake Jeremy. She went to the bathroom and when she emerged, decided she was awake enough to get that glass of water from the kitchen.

Downstairs, she nearly shrieked when she saw Steven leaning against the counter in his robe. The light over the kitchen sink illuminated him as he held his own glass of water in his hand.

"You scared me half to death!" Kathy exclaimed, clutching her chest. "What are you doing up in the middle of the night?"

Steven held up his glass of water. "Needed to cool off."

She stepped beside him and reached for her own glass from the cupboard. "Here's an idea: lose the robe."

"I'd have no objections there, but I don't think your sister would appreciate me strutting my stuff for the whole house to see."

Kathy looked him up and down and made a face. "Ew."

Steven wasn't an unattractive man, but thinking about him in that way led to a slippery slope of thoughts that Kathy did not want imprinted in her mind.

He smiled. "I'm kidding. It's just always been a habit of mine to wear it."

She put up her hand as her glass filled at the sink. "Okay! Conversation is over!"

"I'm glad you're up. I actually wanted to talk to you about Samantha."

Kathy's mind flickered to her conversation with Samantha before she went to bed. Most importantly, what she had said about Steven's mother. "Can we wait to talk until morning? I'm tired."

"It'll just be real quick," he insisted. "Last night on the way home, Samantha told me about your parents. I knew your mother was gone, but I didn't know all the details about your dad."

Kathy averted her eyes and studied her hands. This was not the conversation she expected to have in the middle of the night. "Yeah, but we got through it. Samantha actually sacrificed a lot more than I did to keep things as normal as possible."

"She mentioned something about that," he said. "I brought up how I thought it'd be a good idea for her to track down your dad so the wedding wasn't all my family."

"Steven, I don't think—"

Her glass overflowed and she swore under her breath as she turned the water off. She spilled out the excess water and Steven reached for a paper towel to clean up any water spills.

"I thought I'd talk to you about this." He wiped the counter and handed her an extra piece to wipe down her glass. "You're her best friend and I just want to make sure she has the wedding she deserves because, like you said, she *has* had to sacrifice a lot. She's a hard worker and she deserves to be surrounded by people who love her."

"She's not going to be upset if the bride side is much thinner than the groom's side." Kathy took the sheet and cleaned off her glass. "And I'm not entirely comfortable talking about her behind her back—especially in the middle of the night."

"It's not anything bad," he insisted. "This is supposed to make her happy."

"What exactly are you asking from me?"

"I want you to help me track down your dad and invite him to the wedding."

"Steven…"

"Just hear me out," he said. "Right now, she's going to be walking down the aisle by herself. I know she'd love it if your dad was there. I mean, you guys grew up with him until just a few years ago."

"Which is when he left and hasn't spoken to us or reached out to us in any way since," Kathy said. "Are you sure you want to track him down and bring up all those feelings of abandonment on a day that's supposed to make her happy? Steven, she wants to marry you. She's excited about it. Let's not ruin that by dredging up the past."

"Are you talking about her feelings or yours?" he asked.

She took a bite of her food and didn't say anything. She didn't have an honest answer for him because she didn't know.

"Look, I know family drama is never easy, but we're getting married," he said. "That's important."

Kathy studied him and let out a deep breath. "I'll feel out Samantha and see what she thinks."

His face lit up. "Thank you!"

"I'm not making any promises." She held up a finger to cut

short his enthusiasm. "For what it's worth, I don't think this is a great idea. But this is yours and Samantha's day. Whatever you two want is what we'll do."

"It's Samantha's day," he clarified. "Not mine."

"But listen to me when I say, even if she agrees, it doesn't mean we're going to find him," she warned. "He's been gone for five years and hasn't reached out or responded to any of our attempts to talk to him. At this point, if he doesn't want to be found, he's not going to be found."

CHAPTER 26

- OCTOBER 1976 -

Heather lifted her head from the crappy mattress she counted as a bed. Someone was pounding on the front door and none of the other girls she shared the apartment with seemed to be getting up to answer it.

Groaning from being disturbed, Heather got to her feet and went to see who it was. A peek through the peephole told her nothing. There didn't seem to be anyone on the other side, but they could've also been standing down on the sidewalk, several steps below the view of the peephole.

Opening the door a crack, Heather looked for anyone who might look pissed. The apartment was on Potter Street, only one block up from where the girls worked on Kensington Avenue. While they didn't normally get visitors, it wasn't unusual for one of the girls to bring her catch of the night back to her room to do the deed.

Heather didn't like the fact that random creepy men were coming into her house in the middle of the night, but with the job they all did, she felt like she couldn't say anything. Still, it meant they ran the risk of one of the men coming back for a two-for-one coupon or some other gripe.

They could never be too careful, especially in their line of work.

But there wasn't anyone on the other side of the door. In fact, Heather was about to close it and return to bed when she noticed the note taped to the door.

Closing the front door long enough to pull the chain off, she grabbed the note and then quickly locked it back up afterward.

When she read the note, she couldn't help but smile.

Is a day date breaking the rules? Meet me at the Vine Street Pier this morning. I'll be on The Lady's Cry. *—Dale*

Day dates cost extra—a lot extra. During the day was when she usually slept so she could stay out later to get more dates and make more money at night. Sacrificing a whole evening was going to cost him. But then, Heather knew that Dale would pay so it was worth the trip out.

She called for a cab—splurging because of her anticipated pay day—and took a quick shower before dressing in something she thought Dale would like. Something respectable, but sexy. She opted for a white sweater that revealed her midriff. It was a little skimpy for October, but Dale would keep her warm—yet another charge. A double win for Heather.

By time she was ready to go, the cab had arrived to take her out of this hellish part of the city and to the river where the docks were.

The cab let her out on the street and she walked onto the docks, searching the names of nearly every boat for *The Lady's Cry*. Finally, on the second pier she spotted it: one of the bigger boats in the pier, but still a comparatively small yacht.

Heather had been on a lot of dates, but never on a yacht before.

"Dale?" she called out, hoping he'd come and greet her to confirm she was at the right place.   When she didn't hear any reply, she figured the worst someone could do if she was wrong was tell her to get off their boat. It wouldn't be the first time she got yelled at for being somewhere she shouldn't have been. Memories of her busking days came back to her.

Once on board, Heather heard the distinct roar of the engine come to life.

"Dale?" she called out again, louder this time to be heard over the motor.

Before she could locate the cockpit, she felt the boat start to move. Heather collapsed on the leather bench in the main salon and watched out the window as the marina slowly passed by her.

Hopefully Dale's the one driving, she thought to herself.

Heather decided to investigate and climbed up the stairs that led to the open cockpit.

"Dale, please tell me it's you" she asked as she ascended the stairs.

A woman stood behind the controls, looking out as she maneuvered between the docks and other boats. She directed the yacht out onto the Delaware River.

"Nope, not Dale," the woman said. She was dressed in black pants and a blue flowery top. Her graying hair was pulled back by a white headband. "I'm his wife, though."

Heather made a face. This was a first. "Damn."

"That's all you have to say for yourself?" The woman slowed the speed of the boat and cut the engine. They sat in the middle of the river, too far to reach either shore without swimming. "You think you can steal my husband from me?"

Heather stepped back toward the stairs but Dale's wife followed. "Wait, hold on. He came to *me*, not the other way around."

The woman nodded back behind Heather. "Why don't we go on down and discuss this more privately?"

Hesitantly, Heather turned and led the woman down belowdeck to the main salon, turning the first moment she could to keep the wife in her sight at all times.

Dale's wife stood with her hands on her hips. "So what's this about my husband telling me last night that he's leaving me for some hooker?"

"Hey, I told him that he and I wouldn't work out," Heather countered. "I told him I was just there to fulfill his fantasies and that what we had wasn't real."

"Seems to me he didn't quite get that message," she said. "He's still convinced that life with a whore would be better than life with the woman he's spent the last thirty years with."

"Okay, wait a minute," Heather said. "I only met with your husband three times. If that's enough to steal him away, then clearly you're just not that great of a wife to keep him. Thirty years or not, it really doesn't matter."

The woman charged and pushed Heather to the floor. Heather grabbed the woman's wrists and tried to gain the upper hand, but Dale's wife was surprisingly strong. She broke free of Heather's grip, reached behind her, and pulled out a short knife.

Immediately, Heather backed off and stepped away from her. "Wait, hold on. Let's talk about this. I won't see him anymore, okay? Is that what you want to hear?"

Dale's wife got to her feet, breathing heavily. She waved her hands in Heather's direction, still holding the knife in her palm with her thumb.

You created heartache
by encouraging temptation.

DAVID NETH

For those sins, you will burn
in eternal damnation.

Heather stared wide-eyed as the woman spoke. Her shock only grew more when she felt her body temperature skyrocket as flames consumed her. Heather cried out and reached for the woman. Dale's wife only offered a smug look before turning and walking to the open deck behind the salon. Fanning her hands together, she jumped over the side and dove into the water.

Meanwhile, the flames consuming Heather caught on the leather furniture, then the wall lining. Soon, the rest of the boat went up as well. The whole room was in flame, the smoke billowing and blinding. Her breathing became ragged and her strength was depleted. It wasn't long before her eyes closed and she gave in to her mortality.

CHAPTER 27

Kathy's alarm buzzed on the table beside her bed and she reached up and turned it off. The sun shone bright behind her room-darkening curtains. She wiped the sleep from her eyes and rolled over to wake up Jeremy, but her hand hit the mattress without bumping into him.

She sat up and looked over at the other side of the bed, seeing that it was empty. Looking to the door, she recognized the sound of the shower. He must've jumped the line for the shower since he woke up early.

It had been two days since all four of them were unofficially living together. The growing pains were evident, but neither of the guys complained too much. Jeremy admitted that he'd rather be at Kathy's then at home, which led her down an obsessive rabbit hole of spiraling thoughts, wondering if her insistence that he stay with her for his safety was interfering with the grieving process of his friend.

From what Samantha told her, Steven liked playing house with Samantha, even if he had to endure living with two extra roommates. But the four of them were working it out for now. The girls felt better since the guys were protected. The only time they were alone was when they were at work, or in Jeremy's case, class.

Opening her bedroom door, Kathy noticed that Samantha's was still closed. She decided to take advantage of Jeremy jumping the line and steal a moment in there herself.

She opened the door, hearing the roar of the shower and feeling the mugginess of the hot water as soon as she stepped inside.

"Give me a sec, babe, I'm going to turn on the faucet to wash my face." She leaned over the sink and waited for him to acknowledge her before turning on the water.

Jeremy didn't respond and she heard the slap of water hit the bottom of the tub as he rinsed himself off. A minute later, the water turned off and the curtain swung open. Through the mirror, Kathy got a full view of her future brother-in-law.

She screamed and rushed out of the bathroom, burying her face in her hands, trying everything to get the image out of her mind.

A moment later, Steven opened the door with a towel

around him. "Kathy, what the hell?"

"I'm sorry!" she said with a cringe. She still had her face in her hands, unable to look at him. "I thought Jeremy was in the shower."

"Knock next time!" he grumbled, stepping past her into Samantha's bedroom and shutting the door behind him. On the other side, she could hear him grumble, "I'm glad we came up with a schedule."

Downstairs, when Kathy stepped into the kitchen she was still red in the face. She couldn't wait to get to work and further away from what happened.

Jeremy sat at the kitchen table with an empty cup of coffee, an empty bowl with cereal remnants, and the newspaper splayed out in front of him. By the sink, Samantha leaned against the counter and cradled her own cup of coffee.

"So, did you have a good morning?" she asked with a smirk.

Kathy waved a finger at them both when she noticed Jeremy snicker too. It was nice to see him smiling. She only wished it was for a different reason. "I didn't know Steven was in there. I thought it was Jeremy."

He looked at his watch. "My time slot isn't until after Steven."

"I just woke up! I didn't realize whose turn it was!"

Samantha kept smiling. She didn't ever have this issue,

being the first in line in the morning. "You still could've knocked."

"I know, I know," she said.

Jeremy stood and stepped to Kathy. "I should get up there before it's *your* time slot." He kissed her before stepping out of the room.

After he left, Kathy moved to the coffee pot and poured herself a cup. "This living arrangement isn't working anymore."

"It's never worked." Samantha set her mug down and marched to the kitchen table where Jeremy had just been sitting. "Seriously, your boyfriend is a slob. He couldn't have taken care of these dishes?" She carried them over to the sink and rinsed them with water. "Was that so hard?"

"At least you haven't seen him naked," Kathy said.

Samantha's eyes grew. "You saw Steven *naked*?"

"What did you think I screamed for?"

Samantha let out a deep breath and rubbed her forehead. "We need space from each other. None of us signed up to live together."

"Well, the only way to put an end to this Brady Bunch nightmare is to stop Heather and we need to be able to *find* her first."

With the guys now living with them, it didn't allow the sisters any free time to devise a plan to find and stop Heather. Kathy was the only one who could've had free time without anyone home, but the diner had her working long hours with the summer rush. At least she was getting a lot of hours.

"Have you given anymore thought to telling Steven about us?" Kathy asked.

"Not really." Samantha crossed her arms and looked down at the floor.

"If he knew what we were and who was after us—after *him*—it would give us time to actually figure out what to do," Kathy reasoned. "Maybe he could distract Jeremy for a while and we—"

"I'm not going to tell him I'm a witch and that there's a Siren after him just so he could distract your boyfriend for half an hour." Samantha shook her head. "I don't want to tell him under any duress. He's going to need time to think through it."

Kathy put up her hands in surrender. "Okay. I just thought it'd help."

"Why don't you take a day off to figure out a plan yourself?"

"Sam, I'm making good money, though! They're actually scheduling me!"

"Will that money matter if Heather gets Jeremy?"

You could take a day off too, Kathy thought to herself, but didn't voice it. Samantha's job mattered and it paid most of the bills. Kathy was easily replaceable at her job.

"Fine, I'll call in today and come up with something," Kathy said. "Anything to get some space from all of you people."

"Well, you're going to have to get used to living with Steven,"

Samantha said. "If we're going to be married, I should be the only one who's seeing him naked."

Kathy fired a look in Samantha's direction. "About him, actually."

"What?" Samantha gave her sister a worried look.

"He talked to me the other night…about Dad."

Samantha sighed and crossed her arms, as if she knew what was coming. "What about him?"

"Well, he asked me to track him down."

"I see. And what did you tell him?"

"That I'd talk to you about it," Kathy said.

Samantha ran her tongue over her teeth behind her lips.

"Look, I know your stance on the subject," Kathy went on. "You have no intention of tracking him down. I get that. But I thought I should at least give it some thought because Steven has a point: your family should be at your wedding."

"You're my family," Samantha said. "That's it. Soon Steven will be too, but for now, it's just you."

"You know that's not true."

"It might as well be!"

Kathy looked toward the kitchen door and brought a finger to her lips. "Keep your voice down. I don't want Steven to hear."

"You two didn't have any qualms about talking about me behind my back," Samantha said.

"That was different," Kathy reasoned.

Samantha rolled her eyes. "So you're going to edit my guest

list without even consulting me?"

"I'm consulting you now!"

"And I'm sure you've already started your search."

"No! I decided it wasn't a good idea to invite him, Sam."

"Oh." Samantha was quiet. "How come?"

Kathy shrugged. "Reaching out to him has never worked before. What makes this any different? And even if your wedding *does* make it different, do we really want a relationship with a father who only sees us for special occasions? It's not the way I want to remember Dad, no matter how he left. And I know all of your memories of him are tarnished so that's why I think it'd be best if he not come. I don't think you should add anymore stress to your workload."

"Makes sense."

"Just promise me you won't tell him," Kathy said. "Steven. I'll bring it up to him myself. I don't want you to cave and feel bad only so you can help Steven try to make you feel good. He doesn't fully understand. And he won't. Not until he knows we're witches."

"And I haven't decided when that'll be yet."

"The clock is ticking on that one. You're about to be man and wife. Secrets shouldn't exist between you."

CHAPTER 28

Kathy pulled *The Art of Magic* out from under her bed and flipped to the familiar page of the location ritual. She had called in to work—again gaining strikes against her because of the short notice. Steven and Samantha had both left for work and Jeremy had left for his one summer class. He'd be back in about an hour, so she had limited time.

She quickly read through the list of supplies she needed and went out to the hallway to get them. They kept candles in a cabinet in the hallway between the doors to their bedrooms. Whether for a romantic evening or a spell of some sort, having extra candles all over the house came in handy.

In that same cabinet, she pulled out an antique bowl that had been their mother's. It was wrapped in an old dish towel to keep it from chipping or cracking. They didn't use it often, but at the moment, she didn't want to go down to the kitchen for a regular bowl. This one was big and would allow her to see more in the water.

Carrying it to the bathroom, she filled it with water and set it on the floor on the opposite side of her bed. She carried the candles over and set them in line with north, south, east, and west and lit them each with a match.

She sat with her legs crossed on the floor, closed her eyes, and recited the spell from memory.

I call on the strength of my power.
Show the Siren's face in the water.

The spell would've been stronger with some sort of personal belonging of Heather's or with another witch. Kathy repeated the spell several more times for a little extra *oomph* before she started to see a picture in the water in the bowl.

As the picture took shape, she saw Heather walking down the beach on Presque Isle. There was a thin crowd laying out in the sun, being that it was a Thursday morning. It seemed to be mostly women in the crowd, although Kathy saw a few men there as well. Heather was probably looking for another victim. Hopefully none of those men on the beach would be tempted by her song.

"Kathy?"

She froze when she heard Jeremy's voice and quickly blew out the candles. Closing the magic book, she slid it under her bed and debated what the do with the rest of the makeshift altar, deciding to just leave them. She shot to her feet and flopped on her bed on her stomach, hoping he couldn't see the magical tools on the floor on the other side of her bed.

"Kathy?" he called again just before pushing her bedroom door open.

"Oh, Jeremy, hi," she said, flustered. "What are you doing here? I thought you had class?"

"I told my professor about Paul and she gave me the homework and told me to go home," he said, leaning against the doorway. "I called my house from school and Michael told me that Paul's parents have made the arrangements. Calling hours are tomorrow night. Funeral is Saturday morning."

Kathy crawled off the bed and went to hug Jeremy. "The next few days are going to be rough."

"Yeah," he said. "I want to go home."

Her heart began to race. "Jeremy, I don't know if you're ready—"

"Of course I'm not ready!" he blurted. "I'll never be ready! Am I supposed to just stay here and pretend it never happened? That I never lived there? Just forget about my apartment like it never existed?"

"No, of course not," Kathy said. "I just think that maybe you should wait until after this weekend. Go back to your place on Monday."

That would give them at least a few more days to stop Heather.

"Why are you so insistent on keeping me here?" he argued.

Kathy opened her mouth to respond, but didn't have a good answer for him.

He stepped back into the hall and raised his hands behind his head. "God, Kathy, I feel like you're trying to control me."

She stood in the doorway, putting her hands on either side to keep him from coming in and seeing what he almost walked in on. "I'm not trying to control you—"

"You're constantly telling me what to do, where to go, when to pick *you* up and take you wherever you need to go. I'm tired of it!"

"I'm sorry I'm too broke to afford a car and I need the help of my *boyfriend* to get me where I need to go," she said, knowing it wasn't helping the situation but it made her feel good in the moment.

"You know what? Just leave me alone the rest of the day." He turned and started down the stairs.

"Fine, that'll be easy," she shouted after him.

Turning back to her room, she slammed the door behind her and stopped when she saw the makeshift altar still on the floor. She debated catching a bus and even walking through Presque Isle to find Heather, but quickly shot that idea down. If she took the bus, she would have to walk right by work and risk her boss seeing her. Besides, it took at least half an hour to *drive* all the way around the park. Walking it to get to the beach at the other end of the park was just stupid.

And she hadn't heard the front door close so she knew Jeremy was still downstairs. She didn't want to risk potentially being walked in on during another magical performance and she still needed to come up with a spell or potion to stop Heather. That would have to wait because, despite how she felt about him at the moment, she still needed to protect Jeremy.

CHAPTER 29

Samantha rushed through the front door after work and set her bag and keys on the table beside the door. She saw Jeremy plopped in front of the TV, where he had been for the last couple days every time she came home from work.

"How was work?" Kathy came out of the kitchen, drying her hands with a dish towel. She had been putzing all day, doing everything she could to avoid being around Jeremy for more than to keep an eye on him.

"It was fine. Is Steven here?"

Kathy nodded upstairs. "Got here about fifteen minutes ago. He's upstairs changing out of his work clothes. Why?"

Samantha leaned over the banister and called up the stairs. "Steven! Put something decent on! Cheryl's coming over!"

"Cheryl? Your wedding planner?" Kathy asked.

Samantha nodded. "Yeah, she called me at work just before I left the office and said she had some preliminary questions to go over with us."

"And that can't wait?" Kathy tossed the dish towel over her shoulder and leaned closer to her sister. "I was able to locate Heather this morning with a location ritual. So if we could find her and sneak out with the guys still here—"

"I've been blowing Cheryl off all week because of that," Samantha said as Steven came down the stairs. "She's not going to take no for an answer."

"Who? Cheryl?"

"Yeah, she'll be here in about—" Samantha checked her watch and the doorbell rang. "Now." She looked to Kathy and nodded back to the living room. "Do you mind?"

Kathy sighed. "We've been arguing all day…"

"I'll go let Cheryl in," Steven said, letting the sisters talk.

"Kathy, I'm sorry that things are rough," Samantha said. "But can you please do me this favor and just get him to move to another room?"

She nodded and stepped into the living room, where she turned off the TV. Behind her, she heard Cheryl's booming voice. "There's my favorite couple!"

"Hey! I was watching that!" Jeremy whined to Kathy.

"Sorry." Kathy pushed his feet off the coffee table. "Steven and Samantha have a meeting for their wedding. They're going to use the living room."

Jeremy looked up and Kathy turned around to see Steven, Samantha, and Cheryl all standing in the cased opening looking at them expectantly.

"Will you two be planning your own special day soon?" Cheryl beamed, clearly not reading the mood.

Samantha laughed nervously. "I'm not going to let them steal my thunder." She ushered her to a chair. "Please, take a seat."

"We'll be out of your hair in a minute." Kathy tugged on Jeremy's arm and brought him to his feet. She pulled him out into the foyer.

"You won't be joining us?" Cheryl asked, setting her stack of folders on the coffee table where Jeremy's feet had just been. "Aren't you the maid of honor? And I'm assuming he's one of the groomsmen?"

Steven and Jeremy exchanged glances before the groom-to-be murmured, "Well, we haven't really discussed that."

"I think it'd be beneficial if the wedding party was a part of the planning, don't you?" Cheryl looked between Samantha and Steven. "That way everyone is on the same page."

"Do I have to?" Jeremy asked Kathy quietly.

"Just give us an hour, okay?" she told him.

He rolled his eyes and walked off, grumbling under his breath about her controlling him. Kathy's heart broke for him because she knew there was truth to his words.

"Have a seat! You're making me nervous!" Cheryl opened her folder and pulled out a pad of paper. "Now, we have some decisions that need to be made to help direct me in the planning of it all. Have you narrowed down your choices for bakeries for the cake?"

Steven and Samantha, who were seated together on the couch beside Kathy, looked at each other.

"Um…we haven't—" Samantha started.

"Not really," Steven finished.

Cheryl rifled through her folders and pulled out a sheet of lined paper ripped from a notebook. On it was a list of several bakeries in the area with the phone numbers listed. "I took the liberty of putting together a list of bakeries I've worked with in the past. They're all fantastic, but there are some differences in price. Decide which ones sound the best and I can set up tastings for you. Now, on to the next thing: have you started looking for your dress? Kathy, I'm sure you're chomping at the bit to start shopping!"

Kathy gave a polite smile.

"Not yet," Samantha said. "Honestly, I haven't done much. We've only been engaged for a month."

"I know!" Cheryl exclaimed. "All the time that's already passed! I can't believe we let it get away from us! Now, I'd get on that sooner than later if I were you. I've seen girls who've had to order dresses, have it altered, re-altered, and pressed before the big day. Lots to think about! Lots to do! Thankfully, you have me."

Steven leaned over to Samantha while Cheryl was consulting her notes and whispered, "How much is all of this going to cost?"

Samantha shrugged and whispered back, "We can talk about it later."

Cheryl perked her head up and handed Samantha a glossy magazine. "Here is a catalog of different designers in the Greater Erie area. I'll warn you, just like the bakeries, some are a bit pricey. But can you really put a price on love?"

Samantha passed it off to Kathy, who flipped through it, her eyes bulging at the dollar amounts she saw.

"Now, this next thing I wanted to discuss with you I may be able to help with if you're worried about costs."

"Oh good," Steven said.

"Are you thinking of having a DJ or a wedding singer?"

Samantha again looked to her fiancé and then asked Cheryl, "Do we have to decide all of this now?"

"It's good to get ahead of the game!" Cheryl said. "Especially since you haven't found a venue yet. If you make decisions about other aspects of the wedding, you'll know what to consider when a venue tells you what they will and won't provide. Now, I don't mean to toot my own horn, but I've sung at a few weddings myself. And since I'm already helping you *plan* the wedding, I would offer you a discount if you went with me to entertain the crowd. Do you want to hear a sample?"

She didn't wait for a response and, after singing a few bars on a scale with her forefinger and thumb pinched together, she dove into a rendition of *I Can't Help Falling in Love with You.*

Samantha, Steven, and Kathy were all surprised. Cheryl sounded good. Better than good, she was a terrific singer. The fact that she just started into the chorus in the middle of their living room only added to their awe.

She stopped singing abruptly and said, "That's a popular one for a first dance. Have you thought about what your first dance will be to? Oh, if you want to hear something upbeat—"

Samantha put up her hand to stop Cheryl. "That's okay."

"We'll have to think about," Steven added with a smirk.

Cheryl's shoulders slumped in an exaggerated way. "Ugh, you two are *killing* me! So indecisive! You best start making decisions soon! Otherwise, the soonest you'll be able to get married might be a couple *years* from now."

"Sorry," Samantha said. "Now that we have all of this information, we'll discuss it and get back to you. It's…it's a lot."

"Oh, I know, dear." Cheryl began to pack up her things. "That's why you have me! I'll help in whatever way I can. Now, before I go, I know we discussed earlier this week that you're leaning more toward an indoor wedding now. Somewhere where you can have the ceremony and reception all in one place, right?"

Samantha nodded.

"No church?"

Steven shrugged, as if he would consider it, but Samantha shot it down quickly. "No, we're okay with just a civil ceremony."

The last thing she needed was something magical to happened at the ceremony as they crossed that line between religion and magic.

"Any thoughts on officiants?"

Samantha shook her head. Steven suddenly seemed tenser and she realized it was because she made a decision for the two of them without discussing it first. Even if, in her mind, it wasn't up for discussion.

"Not yet," Samantha said.

"Okay then. We have time for that as well. The biggest thing you need to focus on right now is the venue. I have one in mind that I think would be perfect. Are you free tomorrow around this time? I might be able to arrange a quick tour."

"Tomorrow night I actually have a wake to go to," Kathy said. Jeremy would kill her if she missed it.

"Oh, I'm so sorry," Cheryl said. "I hope it was no one close."

"No, I'm going…for a friend."

"Well, as much as you'd be welcome, as long as the bride and groom are there…"

Samantha looked to Steven for input, but got a stony expression instead. "I would like Kathy there." If, for no other reason, than to make sure nothing fishy happened with Heather while they were distracted in a public place. They needed to stop her sooner than later and taking some time off of work for the wedding planning might be the perfect excuse for more time to deal with Heather. "Maybe we could take tomorrow off and we could do an early afternoon thing. What do you think?"

Steven shrugged. "I could take a half day."

"Excellent!" Cheryl exclaimed. "I'll get it set up and let you know. In the meantime, you two start making decisions! We're going to need answers sooner than later!"

They walked her to the door and bid their goodbyes. The three of them looked at each other once she was gone and took a collective breath. Cheryl was a lot to handle and could only be taken in small doses. That much was understood without a single word exchanged.

"I'm going to go tell Jeremy the coast is clear." Kathy turned and walked off to the kitchen.

Steven crossed his arms and looked at Samantha.

"What?" she asked.

"We never discussed a civil ceremony."

Samantha shrugged. "Neither of us are church-going people. I didn't think it was that big of a deal."

"Just because I don't go to church doesn't mean I'm not religious."

"Well, I'm not, so…" Kathy's voice rang in her head. This would be the perfect time to tell him she's a witch. It would explain her insistence on a civil ceremony. Instead, her fear of his reaction kept her from speaking up. Better to argue about it now and apologize later than to potentially call off the wedding altogether.

"So just like that, that's the decision?" he asked.

"Steven, I don't want to argue about this." She turned and started toward the kitchen, where she heard Kathy and Jeremy swapping barbs. Guess it was that mood in the house today. Not that the forced living arrangements were helping any.

Steven followed and when they got into the kitchen, they caught the tail-end of Kathy and Jeremy's argument.

"…not your little puppet-boy," Jeremy said.

"I'm not trying to control you! I just—"

"Just *what*, Kathy? I want to go home!"

"You don't understand," she pleaded. "You—"

"All right!" Samantha called out and clapped her hands together to get them to listen to her. "That's enough! I get it, we're all a little testy living under one roof. We've all got a lot going on, but we're adults. So let's act like it."

"I don't think giving each other a bit of space is a bad thing," Steven said.

"See!" Jeremy waved his hand in his direction.

"Would you stop?" Kathy snapped. "Like living with me is so bad. You never hear me complaining when you want me to stay at your house for days on end. Or is that because the expectation is that I put out?"

"Okay!" Samantha called out again with another hand clap.

"Maybe we all need a change of scenery. Get some food in us and get to know each other better to work out a better arrangement. Let's all go out to dinner together. Act like a big, happy family."

Everyone grumbled at the idea and Samantha shot her sister a look, who got the message: the better they kept the peace, the better they could protect Steven and Jeremy from Heather.

As much as Kathy herself wouldn't mind space from everyone, she knew that wasn't an option right now. "Where do you want to go?"

CHAPTER 30

Isn't this nice?" Samantha asked once they were seated. Since no one had an opinion on where they wanted to go, Samantha settled on one of the chain restaurants near the Millcreek Mall.

"It's not a pizza on my couch, but sure, it's nice," Jeremy said.

"Don't be a jerk," Kathy said.

"It's my treat," Samantha added. "So order whatever you want."

"Can't I just go home?"

Kathy leaned in to her boyfriend. "You're being rude. Stop it. She's only trying to do something nice."

He sat up and looked right at Samantha. "I'm sorry, you're

right. I guess I'm just bitter because I'm being held against my will."

Kathy rolled her head back and tried to stifle her anger with a deep breath.

Steven picked his head up from his menu. "Jeremy, I'm sorry for your loss and everything you're going through, but please stop dumping it all on Kathy. She's only trying to help."

Samantha put her hand on his arm as a warning, but it didn't work.

"She's trying to help by keeping me away from my house?" Jeremy asked. "Imagine if one of your friends died—maybe even killed—"

Kathy gripped his arm and gave it a gentle squeeze. "You're getting loud," she murmured through gritted teeth. "Knock it off."

"We all know what you're going through," Steven said. "But you have a car. It's parked right in front of mine at the girls' house. Be a grown man and drive yourself home."

"Don't talk down to me," Jeremy said. "I'm not your friend. You made that much clear earlier."

"Jeremy, you're making a scene," Kathy said. "This is embarrassing."

Samantha, who had been watching the whole argument play out and had given up on trying to reconcile the evening, picked her head up when she heard something. A song, at first just barely audible over the chatter of the restaurant, then growing louder.

The Siren's song.

She looked over at Steven, then Jeremy. Her fiancé had stopped arguing and sat up straight, his eyes wide and staring forward. Samantha followed his gaze and saw it was locked on Heather, who was seated at a table by herself in that damned purple dress. Meanwhile, Jeremy continued to bicker with Kathy about what was right for him during his grieving process and who knew best for him.

When Samantha turned her attention back to where Heather had been sitting, she saw that the Siren was walking to the door.

"Hey!" Samantha tried to call after her, but other than a few other diners who looked up, it went unnoticed. "Kathy!" She tried, knowing that her sister's power would stop Heather from escaping, but Kathy was deep in conversation with Jeremy.

Samantha turned and saw Steven's eyes were following Heather out the door. He rose out of his seat and walked across the dining room toward the door. "Steven!" she quietly called for him, knowing it was no use. "Kathy," she barked back at her sister again, before getting up and chasing Steven out of the restaurant.

Kathy looked up and saw the other side of their table had left. She turned and, out the window, witnessed Heather's purple dress flowing in the breeze as she rounded the corner of the building in the parking lot.

Jeremy continued to whine about Kathy with no notice of what happened. She started to look around, debating what to do. She didn't want to leave Jeremy unprotected, but now Steven was being lured away and Samantha would need help stopping Heather.

It was also time for her to realize: the Siren's magic only worked on men in loving relationships and it clearly had no effect on Jeremy.

Throwing her napkin on the table, she raced out the door as Jeremy called after her.

CHAPTER 31

y time Kathy burst through the restaurant doors and raced around to the back of the building, she saw her sister chasing Steven to the back of the parking lot. In the distance, where the lot came to a point and was shrouded among trees that cut off human development from Walnut Creek, Kathy could see Heather's purple dress flowing in the wind.

Breaking into a run, Kathy set off to stop Heather before she could walk away with Steven in tow. As she ran by her sister, she saw Samantha jump on Steven's back to help slow him in his trance. From the look of it, he proceeded unfazed, carrying Samantha with him as he marched toward the Siren.

"Stop!" Kathy called to Heather.

To her surprise, the Siren did stop and turned toward them. Steven—with Samantha on his back—caught up to Kathy and continued on to Heather, who smirked at them and made to turn back to keep going.

Raising her hands, Kathy froze both Steven and Heather in place.

Samantha slid off her fiancé's back and stood next to her sister with her chest heaving. She looked back at the restaurant and then at Kathy. "Where's Jeremy?"

"Still inside," Kathy said, keeping her eyes on the problem that required their immediate attention.

"He didn't hear the Siren's song?"

"No."

Samantha's eyes lingered on her sister for a moment and then she turned her attention back to Steven and Heather. "What are we going to do with them?"

"In the short term, he's safe," Kathy said. "I don't know how long my magic will hold on her, though."

"What were the ways you read that could stop her?"

"Suggestions," Kathy corrected. "And it was to either bind her hands with a rope and then say a spell to kill her, neither of which we have." She looked at Heather's hands, which were on either side of her. Even if they did have rope or string or something, there was no way to bind her hands together.

"What was the other suggestion?"

"To play music that's more beautiful than the Siren's song."

"Isn't that kind of subjective?" Samantha asked. "Whether or not a song is 'good' depends on a person's taste."

"Well, considering Steven is her target, perhaps we need to find a song that *he* finds more beautiful than the one she's singing," Kathy said. "Since you're the only other person who can hear her song, and since you know him better than I do, you should be the one to decide what's more beautiful."

"Even if I knew what song, we have no way to play it," Samantha said. "We're fresh out of options."

"Maybe we should just talk to her," Kathy suggested. Before her sister could object, she raised her hand and unfroze just Heather.

At first, the Siren continued to turn away from them until she noticed Steven was no longer following her and she turned to face the witches.

"What is this? How have you stopped my magic?"

Samantha raised her eyebrows. "Witches have their own tricks too."

"Your hold won't last forever," the Siren countered.

"Leave him alone," Kathy said. "He hasn't done anything to hurt you."

"I hold no grudges against this man," she said. "As I told your sister, my problem is with you both for stopping me from fulfilling my life's work. Going after your men is the only way I can make you pay for what you cost me."

"Leading men to their death is your life's work?" Kathy scoffed.

"Are you upset because my magic revealed something about your own relationship?" Heather asked. "After all, my magic only works on men in love and I only see one man here when I clearly targeted both of them."

Kathy didn't say anything. She could feel Samantha's eyes on her. Feel the questions bubbling under the surface, but nobody said anything for a while.

"It's hard for people to take an honest look at their own lives, isn't it?" Heather went on after a moment.

"We know you're a Siren," Samantha said, hoping that by revealing that bit of information, it would scare Heather into wondering—worrying—what else the sisters knew.

Instead, Heather smirked. "And?"

"We know how to stop you," she lied. Kathy was still staring at the Siren without a word.

"If that were true," Heather said, "you wouldn't be *telling* me to go away. You would be doing it with witchcraft. So no, I don't believe you've quite figured that out."

Samantha gritted her teeth, wishing she had a better retort, but she didn't. She also hoped that Kathy's magic on Steven would hold.

"Well, if that'll be all, I'll let you two have this small victory,"

Heather said. "We all know there will be more attempts. Eventually, I will succeed. You'll be distracted for just a moment too long. Just long enough for him to cross that point of no return, betray whatever love you share, and tarnish the strength of your relationship to the point that it costs him his life. But then, you already know that because you know I'm a Siren." She grinned at the girls.

Neither of them had anything else to say. Samantha wished they had a spell or something. Instead, they just stared at the Siren as she started to turn away.

After taking a few steps, Heather turned back and addressed Kathy. "Oh, and I'm sure you can rest easy, dear. I believe I've done you a favor by showing you just how pointless it is to continue to live out this lie with the man you claim you love. Bye now!" She walked toward the trees lining the edge of the parking lot.

Samantha turned to Kathy and rubbed her arm. "Are you okay?"

Kathy shrugged and a few seconds later, Steven unfroze.

He looked around, confused. "Did we finish dinner?"

"Um…" Samantha looked between Steven and Kathy. "We decided to skip dinner."

"Where's Jeremy?" he asked.

Samantha and Kathy looked at each other before the older sister said, "He needed some space."

CHAPTER 32

- OCTOBER 1976 -

Soft, persistent beeping woke Heather. She looked up at the various monitors beside her bed. Tubes and cords running from the machines to different places on her body.

The last thing she remembered, she was burning on a boat on the river. So how did she get here? How was she alive? And how did her strength seem to be growing with each passing minute?

"Ah, Miss Doe, you're awake." A male nurse in blue scrubs walked into her room and looked her over. His smile was bright and genuine, which immediately captured her attention.

"Miss Doe?" Heather asked.

"We didn't know your name, so we called you Jane Doe,"

he explained. "Now that you're awake, you can tell us your real name."

"Oh?" She smirked. "And what do I get for revealing all of my secrets?"

The nurse smiled. "You get my full cooperation to help get you out of here and back home. Not that I want to see you go."

Heather pinched her gown and lifted it slightly. "I'm sure you've seen everything under here. Anything you like?"

He chuckled and raised his left hand, which brandished a wedding ring. "I'm married, but I appreciate your enthusiasm. You're a pistol."

The realization that he was married seemed to captivate Heather. She had an overwhelming urge to sing—something she hadn't wanted to do in years. Not since she started working the streets.

"Do you like music?" she asked.

"Love it," he said. "You into pop stuff or more rock'n'roll?"

"I have my own style that I'm partial to." She began singing, meeting his eyes and locking him in with her voice.

The nurse stared at her, captivated. He leaned in closer to Heather with desire in his eyes that wasn't there before.

Heather watched in amazement, but continued to sing. Something inside her told her she had to keep going. This was what fulfilled her now.

Leaning even closer, the nurse pressed his lips against hers and immediately started to convulse and shake. When they parted, smoke escaped his lips, followed by flame, which burned from his heart and spread to the rest of his body. He collapsed on the floor as smoke filled the room.

Heather got to her feet and looked down at him burning, a smile spread across her face. She wiped saliva from her lips and felt a sense of satisfaction and vindication. Any man who cheated on his wife deserved to be punished, just as she was for sleeping with a married man.

She pulled the wires and cords off of her and rushed out of her hospital room, eager to find more adulterous men.

CHAPTER 33

The first thing Kathy did when they got back to the house was call Jeremy's house. He didn't wait for them at the restaurant after they encountered Heather and the whole way home, Kathy worried that maybe he had been targeted by Heather after all. The fact that his car was still in their driveway only heightened her worry.

"Yeah, he's here," Michael told her once she got through.

"Oh good." Kathy leaned against the wall in the kitchen and twirled the phone cord around her finger.

"I guess he took the bus. He didn't really say much when he got home."

"I'm not surprised."

"Do you want to talk to him?"

Kathy considered it. She wanted to yell at him for embarrassing her in public, but at the same time she knew she was pushing him too far at a time when he needed time to process. And what good would come of arguing on the phone? They both needed space. After what the Siren pointed out about their relationship, there was a lot she needed to think about.

"No, that's okay," she finally said. "He probably doesn't want to talk to me anyway."

"Are you guys okay?"

"I'm not sure yet," she said. She worried that the state of their relationship was dead in the water.

"Oh."

"Yeah. How are you doing?"

He sighed. "Okay, I guess. It's still shocking to think about, but Maddie's helping me through."

Kathy felt a twang of pain in her chest. She didn't help Jeremy through anything. She was too distracted about keeping him safe from the Siren that she didn't focus on being his girlfriend. Someone he needed, especially right now.

"That's good." She tried to keep the emotion out of her voice. "Hey, look, I gotta run. Take care of Jeremy, will you? He needs...he needs a friend."

"I will," he said. "Are you going to the calling hours tomorrow? Or the funeral?"

She paused and considered it. It would definitely be a way to make up for being a lousy girlfriend all week to Jeremy. But she didn't want to start a fight and cause a scene at an event like that. "I don't know yet."

"We'd all love to see you there," Michael said. "Please think about it."

"We'll see. Call me if anything comes up with Jeremy."

"We'll take care of him. But I'll keep that in mind."

Samantha walked into the kitchen as Kathy hung up the phone.

"Jeremy made it home." Kathy leaned forward on the counter.

Samantha opened the refrigerator door and pulled out several bags of luncheon meat. "That's good."

"I suppose."

"Did you want to go over there and get him so you know he's safe?" She grabbed the bread and pulled out two slices. "I'm making a sandwich because we missed dinner. Do you want one?"

"No, I'm okay," Kathy replied. "And no, I don't think going to get Jeremy is going to help anything anyway. If what—" She stopped and looked to the door. "Where's Steven?"

"Watching TV. Baseball or something, I don't know." Samantha looked down at her spread. "Oh, I should probably make him one too…" She pulled out two more slices of bread.

"Anyway, if what Heather said was true, then I have nothing to worry about with Jeremy."

Samantha replaced the bread and opened the fridge for the

mayo. "What do you mean?"

"We confirmed it in the book, even. The Siren's magic only works on men in love with the women they're committed to. Jeremy never heard the Siren's song, so…" She shrugged.

Coming around the island, Samantha gave her sister a sideways hug. "I'm sorry. I wish there was an easier way for you to have figured that out, but no matter how you did, it still wouldn't have been easy."

"I know." Kathy squeezed her sister's hand on her shoulder. "I'll be okay. I think I've known for a while now, just didn't want to admit it to myself."

Samantha returned to making her sandwich, grabbing a knife from the drawer on the way. "The heart has a way of knowing."

"Yeah. Anyway, we need to come up with a plan to stop her. Steven is still very much a target."

"Tell me about it. But unless we find a way to bind her hands—and I'm sure she knows that's a weakness of hers—or if we suddenly become opera singers who sound more beautiful than the Siren, we're running low on options."

"I think our best bet is to hope we can get her hands bound, but plan to overpower her song," Kathy said.

"How are we going to do that?"

"Your wedding planner has a great voice."

Samantha nodded as she finished making hers and Steven's sandwiches. "True, but how are we going to get her to sing for us to stop Heather without telling her we're witches?"

"Well, I've been thinking about that and I have an idea."

"Care to share?"

"I'm going to have to come up with several spells and we'll have to time it right, but it should work." Kathy dove into her idea, talking quickly and countering all of Samantha's devil's advocate arguments.

When she finished, Samantha looked at her sister and said, "You're right. The timing will be key. To stop Heather and to keep from exposing ourselves. Here's another caveat: how are we going to find her? Up until now, she's just shown up whenever we're with the guys. And even then, that's not always the case."

"I've been thinking about that," Kathy said. "I'm starting to remember some of the mythology of Sirens. They are typically known to be creatures who stay close to bodies of water. Sailors, for instance, were historically their targets."

"I'm sure most sailors didn't stay loyal to their wives, if they had them, so that makes sense."

"Right," Kathy said. "Obviously, over the years Sirens have evolved, just like witches have. I mean, we're not necessarily sweeping from east and west to spark magic anymore. We have it at our fingertips. But things like talismans and herbs and potions are still a part of our craft."

"This is all very fascinating, Kathy, but how does this help us find Heather?"

"I'm saying, what if Sirens still follow some of their traditional patterns?"

"I'm still not following."

"Think about where we've encountered Heather in the past week."

Samantha took a bite of her sandwich as she thought. "Um…at Presque Isle. I saw her on the pier. You saw her at the diner and then we both saw her by the mall. I don't see how any of those have anything in common."

"They're all near bodies of water."

"They are?" Samantha scrunched her eyebrows together and took another bite.

"Obviously, Presque Isle and the pier are both by Lake Erie, that's an obvious one. The diner is just about four blocks away from Fourmile Creek, which runs right into the lake. Even where we went for dinner today, the back of the parking lot butts up against Walnut Creek, which meanders a bit but ends up in the lake."

"So you're saying she's traveling by water?"

"Somehow, yes," Kathy said. "At least that's my theory. We even need to be careful here at the house because Mill Creek cuts right through the neighborhood. Although, I doubt she would attack us here, being our home turf and all."

"So do you think she has a boat or something?"

Kathy shrugs.

"A boat," Steven said as he walked through the door. Both

sisters jumped. "With this heat, I'd love to take a day on a boat."

"Me too," Kathy said quickly. Through the years, the girls had grown accustomed to quickly redirecting their conversations away from magical topics. "We might be able to rent one on Presque Isle."

"And probably pay a fortune," he added.

Samantha slid him his sandwich, which was on a paper towel. "Here, I made this for you."

"Thanks." He leaned over and kissed her cheek. "Have you heard from Cheryl yet about her plans for us tomorrow?"

"Not yet," Samantha said. "I'm still debating on everything she wanted us to think about. We can talk about it tomorrow morning if you want." Before they left for dinner, they both called their bosses to take the following day off. Samantha only wished she really had the whole day to plan the wedding, but she knew a portion of it would be devoted to her witch responsibilities.

He sighed. "Can I be honest? I'm already tired of all the wedding planning."

Samantha made a face. "I'm sorry, honey. I'll try to take care of most of it, but I want you there to make some decisions too."

Steven shook his head. "Don't worry about it. Just plan the wedding you want. If you're happy, I'll be happy."

"Aw," Kathy couldn't help but say as the two kissed.

Samantha rolled her eyes at her sister.

Steven turned to head out of the kitchen. "I'm going back to watch TV. You guys want to watch a movie later?"

"Look in the *TV Guide* and see what's on," Samantha said. "We'll be there in a minute."

He nodded again and disappeared out of the room.

"He's great," Kathy said. "You're lucky."

"I know. I just feel bad about dragging him through my bridezilla craziness."

"For what it's worth, you've calmed down a lot," Kathy said. "I'm not even annoyed with you about it anymore."

"Funny how a Siren threatening the life of my fiancé helps put things into perspective, isn't it? I don't know, I just don't have the same motivation as I did when we were first engaged."

"Are you having second thoughts about the wedding?"

"No, that's not it. With all of this going on—with Steven getting almost hypnotized by Heather and almost walking off to his death—it just makes me wonder why I'm bothering with the big hoopla. I mean, all I need is that man out there. Even without the dress and the flowers and the cake and the guests, I'll be content as long as he's there."

Kathy smiled. "That's not a bad thing. Maybe you should scale down the wedding, then."

"I know."

"Have you given anymore thought to telling him you're a witch? That might help relieve some of your stress. I mean, you *are* lying to him. It'd be nice if we could talk openly. Especially if he's going to be living here."

Siren

Samantha stared out the door where Steven had just exited. "I know I have to, but I just…want to wait for the right time, you know?"

"You can't keep putting it off. Like I said before, the sooner the better."

Tears pooled in Samantha's eyes and she looked down at the crumbs leftover from their sandwiches. She gave an involuntary sob and her shoulders shook.

Kathy came around the island to give her sister a hug. "Oh, honey, what's the matter?"

Samantha wiped at her eyes, even though more tears kept spilling out. "I'm just afraid of what he'll say."

"He loves you," Kathy said. "That's what he'll say."

"But what if he doesn't want to marry me because I'm a witch? What if that's just too much for him to handle? It's a big ask. I mean, he's already been in danger several times because of it and he didn't even know it. How could I expect him to be okay with a lifetime full of that?"

Kathy squeezed her sister tighter because she didn't have an answer. Not a good one. They both hoped that the men they'd one day marry would understand, but what if they didn't? What if both sisters were destined to be alone?

CHAPTER 34

The next day, Samantha put the car in park in the mostly-empty parking lot of the Sunset Inn. It was a modest-looking building tucked away in a suburban-style residential area on the edge of the city, perched on a ledge overlooking Lake Erie.

In the car, Steven was in the passenger seat and Kathy was sitting in the back. There were only two other cars in the parking lot. One of which, Cheryl climbed out of and waved exuberantly to them with a clipboard in her other hand held against her chest.

"Honey, why don't you go greet Cheryl?" Samantha said to Steven. "I want to talk to Kathy about something real quick."

He looked between the two of them and unbuckled his seat belt. "Okay."

SIREN

"We'll just be a second," she added. "Don't get started without us!"

They watched as he crossed the front of the car over to where Cheryl stood by hers. Steven and Cheryl both looked back at Samantha's car in confusion before quickly turning their attention to the venue. Under the copse of the trees, it really was beautiful.

Kathy leaned forward from the backseat with a piece of paper in her hand. "You ready to put this plan into action?"

Samantha huffed out a breath. "As ready as I'll ever be. Is this the first spell?"

"Yeah. You ready?"

The older sister nodded and together, they both recited:

> *Your voice, your song,*
> *your beautiful gift,*
> *Make it one that*
> *Steven can't resist.*

They watched as a brief light came over both Steven and Cheryl, who paused their conversation for only a fraction of a second as the spell took effect.

"Do you think it worked?" Kathy asked.

"Hopefully we didn't just cast a love spell," Samantha murmured as she unbuckled herself as well.

"We don't specialize in that kind of magic," Kathy said. "At most, it'll make her voice put him into something like a drunken stupor. As long as it keeps him from being led away by the Siren."

They climbed out of the car.

"That's reversible, right?"

"Shh, don't worry," Kathy muttered as they joined Steven and Cheryl by the door.

"Ugh, isn't this place *beautiful*!?" Cheryl gushed. "Samantha, I thought of you immediately! This place is the best of both worlds for what you're looking for. *Gorgeous* inside venue, a gazebo and patio out back overlooking the lake for your ceremony and pictures. Plus, the trees keep the wind down so it won't mess up your hair on your big day. I think this might be the place!"

"Well, let's see then," Samantha said, trying to squash her nerves now that their plan was in action. If Kathy's theory was right, being near a body of water—especially one as large as the lake—would hopefully draw Heather out on her own. Samantha only hoped they were ready for her like they'd prepared.

"Larry is already inside." Cheryl led them to the front door, only lowering her clipboard when she held the front door open for them. "He's the owner and will be giving us a tour and going over all of the packages that are available if you decide this is the place. I have a good feeling!"

They stepped inside a white formal hallway that stretched the length of the building. To the left was a door to the kitchen and further up the hall on the same side were doors leading to the bathrooms and a small banquet room.

"Over here." Cheryl led them through double doors on the right into a banquet room that took up the whole right half of the building.

Samantha's eyes immediately went to the large stone fireplace on one end of the room. Very quickly, her attention turned to the sun shining on the lake through the windows on the adjacent wall.

"Oh wow," she said without realizing it.

"Amazing, isn't it?" Cheryl gushed.

"That does look nice," Steven added.

"The best part about this place is you have options!" Cheryl moved over to the fireplace. "Image getting married in front of this!" She waved to the window overlooking the patio and gazebo near the lake. "Or outside!"

An older gentleman in a blue blazer and matching pants walked in and smiled at them. He extended his hand to Steven, who stood closest to the door, and said, "I'm Larry, the owner of the Sunset Inn. You must be the groom!"

Steven shook his hand and nodded. "How could you tell?"

"Just a hunch." He gave him a wink. "And which is your bride?"

Samantha stepped forward and extended her hand. "Nice to meet you. I'm Samantha and this is my sister, Kathy. She's going to be my maid of honor."

He greeted her as well and Kathy said, "This is a beautiful place."

"You haven't seen the best yet," he said with a genuine smile. "Wait until you go outside!"

"Let's go!" Cheryl cheered. "I'm just *dying* to get out there!"

"Right this way." Larry led them through the doors and out onto a wooden patio just off the back of the building.

While several trees still towered over them, there was enough of a clearing to have a good view of the lake and to even feel the breeze blowing off of it.

"Is this gazebo where you hold ceremonies?" Cheryl asked, pointing to the structure nearly twenty feet away from the patio.

"Yes, let's go have a look," Larry said.

As they wandered toward the gazebo, Samantha and her sister held back. They looked at each other and Samantha asked, "Ready for spell number two?"

Kathy nodded and waited for Samantha to catch up with Steven and the rest of them before pulling out the paper and reading the spell—another one she crafted the night before— quietly to herself.

Siren, Siren, across the waters.
I call you now to heed my powers.
Come to me at this shore,
To finally settle the score.

SIREN

Kathy looked up when nothing immediately happened. The rest of her group was still gathered in the gazebo, looking out to the water. Only Samantha kept turning back to look at her sister, silently trying to convey whether or not the spell had been cast.

The younger sister nodded and slowly walked toward the gazebo, continually looking around for any sign of Heather. She didn't like feeling like they were about to get ambushed.

Just before Kathy stepped off the back patio, a voice asked, "Looking for me?"

She jumped and spun around to see Heather standing only a foot away. More beautiful than Kathy ever realized.

"I dreamt of a day like the one your sister is planning." She looked down at her dress. "My day never came, which is why I'll never wear white. Among other reasons." She laughed to herself.

"We want you to leave Steven alone."

Heather smirked. "Gave up on Jeremy, did you?" She gave a shrug. "Meh, it's probably for the best. Most men are trash anyway. Now, your sister has seemed to have snagged a good one. But he's been tempted in the past. Let's see if he's tempted again." She began to sing.

"Don't!" Kathy shouted, but still the Siren sang on.

CHAPTER 35

Like I said, you can't beat this view!" On the gazebo looking out toward the lake, Cheryl continued to gush. She turned to look at Samantha and something caught her eye. "Who is that talking to your sister?"

Steven and Larry both turned to look back at the patio as well.

"Oh, just a friend," Samantha said quickly, stepping to the side to try to block their view. She pointed out to the lake. "But *this* is amazing! Couldn't get this downtown, that's for sure! Or even on Presque Isle."

"I *know*!" Cheryl said, staring at the lake with Larry.

Steven seemed to keep trying to look back at who Kathy was talking to. "I've seen that woman bef—"

Siren

"Don't!" Kathy shouted from behind them.

The group began to turn back to the patio, but Samantha started talking quickly to distract them.

"I do have a question," she said. "If we had a wedding singer who was singing as we walked down the aisle—" Behind her, she could hear the Siren's song begin. "—would her voice be washed out with the sound of the lake?"

Steven stepped off the gazebo and started walking back to the patio. To the source of the Siren's song. Her magic was taking effect.

Larry shook his head. "Oh, I don't think you'll have a pro—"

"Cheryl, why don't you close your eyes, imagine we're at the wedding, and sing as if there's a crowd straining to hear you sing," Samantha suggested. "Make sure to keep those eyes closed! Larry, you too! Let's pretend!"

They both looked confused and Samantha chanced a look back at her fiancé, who was almost to the steps of the patio.

"Come on, try it!" Samantha pushed.

"Okay…" Cheryl cleared her throat and began to sing.

CHAPTER 36

As Cheryl started singing, Steven's march toward the Siren stopped. He turned and looked back at the gazebo to hear Cheryl sing. Only then did the Siren's own song falter. Kathy could hear that Heather went only slightly out of tune at first before the perfection of her voice worsened as Steven continued to pay more attention to Cheryl than Heather.

"Not such a good Siren, then, are you?" Kathy asked.

Heather scowled at her, clenched her fists, and tried harder to sing better, louder, than Cheryl. But the spell the witches had cast on Cheryl and Steven was working, confusing Steven in his trance and faltering the Siren's song.

Kathy watched as Samantha jumped from the gazebo and ran to the patio, swerving around Steven on her way. He remained oblivious to her, continually enraptured by Cheryl's voice.

Just as Samantha stepped back onto the patio, the Siren's song stopped completely. Kathy only caught that last glimpse as the familiar purple dress disappeared around the corner of the building.

"Oh no you don't," Kathy muttered as both sisters chased after the Siren.

Out in the parking lot, Heather had nowhere to hide. Kathy put up her hands and froze the sinister songstress in her tracks when the two sisters closed the distance between them.

"You have spell number three?" Samantha asked.

"Right here. Hopefully this works as well as the other two." Kathy pulled another piece of paper from her pocket and straightened it out for both of them to read together.

It's apparent that
Your song's gone flat.
You were once the best,
But put it to rest.
Your magic has failed here,
So go and disappear!

The Siren unfroze and her body quickly distorted as the witches' magic took effect. Her limbs flailed and her spine bent at an unnatural angle until suddenly, her whole body erupted into water and dispersed onto the sidewalk, leaving a puddle.

The sisters looked at each other and smiled until a scream erupted from the back.

Breaking out into a sprint, the sisters came around to the back of the building. They just caught sight of Cheryl slapping Steven across the face and pushing him away, rushing to get away from him. Larry gave him a disgusted look and chased after Cheryl.

"Oh shoot, that spell," Samantha said.

"We must've created a small Siren-like experience with it," Kathy said.

When the sisters approached, they asked what happened.

"Your *groom* tried to make a move!" Cheryl clutched at her chest, which was heaving. Her eyes bulged and she stared at Steven like her had committed a capital offense.

"I'm so sorry," Samantha said, trying her best to hide a smirk. If nothing else, all of this proved just how much Steven loved her. The Siren's magic and the sisters' spell wouldn't have worked if he didn't.

"Young lady, this is something to think about before you get married," she scolded.

"I know, but—" She stopped. There was no plausible explanation for this. She could pretty much count on the fact that Cheryl would no longer be helping them with planning the wedding. Worse, the chances of them booking this venue for the wedding were probably ruined too.

With those thoughts, Samantha wasn't worried or anxious. Instead, she was relieved.

CHAPTER 37

Kathy parked Samantha's car in the parking lot of the funeral home on Pine Avenue in an area that used to be filled with German immigrants. Steven and Samantha were having a much-needed uninterrupted date at the house, so Samantha's car was free for as long as Kathy wanted it.

She stepped out of the car and followed the crowd across the blistering asphalt to the main entrance of the funeral home.

With the sweltering heat, Kathy tried to choose the best black outfit that would also keep her cool. However, "heat" and "black" didn't really blend together. Unless she wanted to don her "little black dress," she was stuck with her only other option: black pants and a dark blue top. Not that she ever really had occasions to wear clothes like these except when someone died or got married.

The end of the line began just outside the door. Luckily, under the awning, which allowed a little relief from the heat, although the humidity made sure she was still sweating. She could feel the gentle breeze of an oscillating fan just through the doorway. Only a few more steps and she'd be inside.

Kathy stretched as far as she dared while still keeping her place in line to double-check that she was in the right line, but the sign just inside had a picture of Paul and an arrow pointing to the correct room.

When someone young dies unexpectedly, it brings a crowd, she thought to herself.

Looking around at the other people who came to pay their respects, she noticed so many people her age as well as middle-aged people. Likely Paul's friends and their families.

With the somber environment, it was hard for Kathy to think that only a few hours ago, she and her sister were facing off with the Siren, who was the cause for all of this. Even if she was dead, the havoc she wreaked still lingered.

Kathy waited for a long time in the line, slowly working her way past several of the checkpoints she set for herself to pass the time. In the door, where she selfishly sucked up every moment with the fan as she could; in the room, where she could finally see the casket adorned with flowers and posters propped up on easels with photo collages; and to Paul's family, who cried and hugged her even though she hadn't ever met them.

After she paid her respects at the casket, Kathy scanned the crowd for Jeremy or any of his friends. Her eyes finally locked on Maddie, who offered her a sad smile and waved her over.

She received an awkward hug from Maddie. The two of them had never been close, but grief made people do things out of the ordinary.

"I'm glad you came," she said.

"Of course." Kathy looked up and noticed Michael and Becky and…Jeremy.

Michael and Becky each gave her a hug. She got only a half-hearted smile from Jeremy. At least it was something.

"How long have you guys been here?" Kathy asked, trying to find something to say.

"We were here right when it started," Maddie said. "Do you want to sit down?"

Kathy's eyes flicked over to Jeremy and then back to Maddie. She held up the envelope she brought. "I should probably just stick this in the box and head out."

They all nodded, as if understanding. She wondered what Jeremy told them about their argument the night before—*if* he told them anything.

Becky pointed by the door. By the looks of it, her tears had long-since wiped away whatever makeup she had applied. She looked tired and drawn out. Not that Kathy could blame her.

"There's a box over by the guest book," she told Kathy.

"Make sure you sign it."

Kathy nodded. "It was nice seeing you all."

They all replied in kind, except Jeremy, who avoided eye contact with her.

She turned and deposited the card among the stack of others before adding her name to the long list of guests. When she was finished, she turned and started for the door. She managed to get two steps forward before she felt someone grab her arm. Turning, she saw it was Jeremy.

"Oh, hi," she said.

"Do you have a minute?" he asked. "I think we need to talk about some things."

"Uh, sure."

He nodded to the door. "Want to take a walk around the block or something?"

"Sure," she said.

He led them outside, back into the blistering heat and out to the sidewalk on Marvin Avenue, where most of the trees had been cut down to make way for power lines and had never been replaced. Kathy could feel the sweat rolling down her back again.

"Listen, I know I've been a horrible girlfriend this week and I just want to say I'm sorry," Kathy started. "I'm sorry you lost your friend and I'm sorry I wasn't as supportive as I should've been."

Jeremy nodded. "Thanks."

"I guess part of it was that lately I've been feeling under appreciated in this relationship and I was demanding more from you at the worst time."

"Under appreciated?" He raised his eyebrows and looked at her. "How were you under appreciated?"

"Jeremy, what did our dates consist of? Going to your house, having sex, and then watching you play video games. Or going to the diner and talking to *your* friends."

"You didn't seem to have any problems with my friends back there when you were hugging them!" he countered.

"Yes, I like them, they're good people, but I thought I was dating *you*, not them. That means, when I go over to your house, I'm there to see you. That means, we need to have some alone time. That means, there needs to be some give and take. So while I worry about finding rides to come over to *your* house, the least you can do is wake up and take me to work like you promised!"

"You know how incredibly selfish you're being? My friend just died!"

"And I'm talking about the way you were acting *before* he died," she said. "This is not a new problem, Jeremy. This is something I've been feeling for a while now."

"Then why didn't you say anything?"

"I thought we could fix it. Why do you think I was insisting on a change of pace? You come to my house instead of staying at yours. Spending time with my sister and Steven instead of always being with your friends."

They were coming up Holmes Street now, almost back to Pine Avenue where the funeral home was.

"Jeremy," she said in a softer voice. "We both have a lot going on right now and this tension between us, which has been a long-time-coming, hasn't helped any."

"So why don't we take a break?" he asked suddenly.

She stopped on the sidewalk and looked at him. "What?"

"We should take a break," he repeated. "You know, break up. If we're not happy with each other, then what are we doing?"

Kathy swallowed the lump forming in her throat and nodded. It's not like she hadn't thought about it herself, but hearing the words made it real and that scared her.

"Yeah, you're right." She continued walking with him, hooking around the corner onto Pine Avenue and approaching the parking lot. "It's just hard to let it go."

"I know," he said. "But maybe this will be for the best. And who knows what the future holds?"

They got to the row where she parked Samantha's car and she motioned to it. "Well, this is me."

They studied each other a moment, as if waiting for the other one to say that they shouldn't break up. But they both knew this was the best option for them.

Finally, Jeremy said, "Goodbye, Kathy."

She reached up and gave him a hug, ignoring the discomfort of their sweaty bodies, and just held him. Squeezed him. When she pulled away, he looked as if he was about to say something, but nodded at her again and turned back to head into the funeral home. Kathy watched him for a moment before turning and going back to Samantha's car, where she cried once she was alone inside.

CHAPTER 38

I must say, it is nice to finally be alone with you." Steven brought in the plate piled high with sausages he had just pulled off the grill.

"Mm-hmm," Samantha murmured as she reached for the paper plates from the cupboard. Her hands were shaking. Their alone time meant that this was the perfect opportunity to tell Steven she was a witch. Kathy was right, the longer she put this off the harder it would be for Steven to process.

"You know, it's not too bad outside." He set the plate on the kitchen island. "Do you want to have a picnic out in the yard?"

"Sure." She tried to sound casual, but his lingering look told her that she was failing in that endeavor. "Why don't you pull out a sheet from the linen closet upstairs? I'll get everything else ready."

"Okay." He kissed her cheek and then disappeared out of the room.

She dug through the back of the pantry and found their old wooden tray. It probably could've used a good washing but then, they were planning on eating in the grass so how clean was this meal going to be anyway?

When Steven returned with the sheet, he held the door open for Samantha as she carried the tray outside, balancing everything on it. He laid out the sheet in the shade of the large oak tree in the corner of the yard and the two of them got situated, dishing out plates and digging in.

"So are we back to square one with the wedding now that Cheryl has officially given us the boot?" he started before taking a bite of his sausage. He tucked the mouthful into his cheek and added, "I wasn't coming on to her or anything...I don't really know what happened."

Well, there's a perfect segue to introduce the idea of her being a witch: an explanation. Something she was so accustomed to avoiding.

"Yeah, about that—"

"Do you mind if we *don't* have a wedding planner? I didn't realize how expensive everything was and then when she was going over all the costs and everything it was...yeah."

"That's fine. I think I've decided on having a smaller

wedding anyway. Honestly, I got carried away with the whole wedding planning thing. It wasn't me and I'm sorry I dragged you into it."

"Don't be. I want you to have the wedding you've always dreamed of…on a budget."

She laughed, which helped her relax a little. "Maybe Kathy and I can plan something together."

"I'm sure my mother would love to help too," he said.

Samantha bristled at that idea, but didn't offer any objections. Mary Harper was going to be her mother-in-law, they needed to get along.

"It's funny how this week turned out, isn't it?" he went on.

"What do you mean?" Samantha wondered if this really was the perfect opportunity to bring up being a witch. After all, the conversation kept shifting away from the perfect moments.

No. She wasn't going to back away from this. She needed to tell him and she needed to do it soon.

"With the four of us living together," he explained. "It was…interesting."

"Like my sister walking in on you in the shower?"

"That wasn't ideal," he said with a snicker. "No, I meant that for such a big house, it was quite crowded with four adults living under one roof."

"Well, we were four adults who didn't necessarily *decide* to live under one roof," Samantha said. "We were kind of forced because—"

"It was kind of fun, but kind of like teenaged, college-aged fun, you know? And if we're going to be married, I think we're growing out of that, aren't we?"

"I mean, I guess," Samantha said, not sure where he was going with this. "But Kathy and I live together because—"

"Because you two own the house together, yeah, I know. But the house is paid for. All that's left is insurance, taxes, and utilities."

"Right…" Samantha looked at him skeptically.

"So in theory, we could help Kathy out if she's struggling, but for the most part, she might be able to handle it on her own."

Samantha closed her eyes and pinched the bridge of her nose. "Wait, Steven, what are you talking about?"

"I'm talking about us getting our own place once we get married," he said.

"You mean, separate from this house?"

"Well, yeah. If we're going to get married and have kids someday, we're going to need our own space."

"And this large house is perfect for that," she said.

"So you're going to ask Kathy to get her own place?"

"Why does anyone have to move out?" she asked. "We're getting married, that doesn't mean we need to disown anyone."

"I didn't say we'd disown her," Steven said. "But if we're married, we need our own space. You see how that could be an advantage, right?"

"Well…yeah."

Siren

"Look, I'm not saying it's an absolute. I'm just saying it's something to seriously consider. We have time before anything needs to happen. Just promise me you'll think about it, okay?"

She met his eyes. Saw how genuine they were. He was excited about their *marriage* while she had been focused on their *wedding*. She couldn't blame him for that and the thought of him considering their future together made her happy.

Finally, she nodded and said, "Okay. I'll think about it."

Samantha's mind was spinning. She knew she and Kathy wouldn't live together forever, but she couldn't imagine living in a place where her sister wasn't just in the next bedroom. But Steven was going to be her husband. Changes were coming, whether she was ready for them or not.

The valkyries secretly hand-select fallen heroes to bring back to Valhalla to prepare for the final battle. While out at a nightclub, Kathy witnesses a valkyrie collect a dying man's soul. Thinking the valkyrie is doing harm, she tries to fight her off, but loses.

Back in Valhalla, the valkyries view their lapse in secrecy as a sign that the final battle is beginning. They capture Kathy and bring her back to Valhalla while they rally their army to send into battle.

Meanwhile, Samantha is reeling from having told Steven she's a witch. But when she discovers Kathy's gone missing, she puts her strained relationship aside to save her sister, only to end up in just as much danger as Kathy.

With the valkyries preparing for war, Samantha and Kathy must prove that they mean no harm in order to return to their normal lives. But the end of the world might be sooner than they think.

Valkyrie is the third book in the Coven series, which serves as a prequel series to the Under the Moon series.

VALKYRIE

COVEN: BOOK 3

Read on for an excerpt of the next book in
the Coven series!

DAVID NETH

CHAPTER 1

- AUGUST 1988 -

I realize helping me set up our romantic date isn't exactly romantic." Samantha grabbed two corners of the green tablecloth with a glittering floral pattern weaved in with a darker shade of green.

Steven grabbed the opposite two corners and helped fan it out over the table. "Who says perfection is romance?" With the tablecloth now covering the table, Steven ambled to Samantha and hooked his arm around her while she straightened it out. "I have you, a delicious meal, and the house to ourselves."

Heels clunked on the hardwood, as if on cue. Moments later, Kathy came down the stairs in a tight red dress.

"You'll be by yourselves in two minutes." She pulled at the hem to cover up more of her legs, then dug through her clutch.

"I'm going downtown again tonight. I'll be home late, so don't wait up."

Samantha stared wide-eyed at her sister. "Kathy, you look—"

"Amazing, I know." Kathy smiled and then moved to the mirror in the foyer and applied her lipstick.

"I mean, it's a little revealing," Samantha said. "Are you even comfortable? You look like you're going to pop out."

Kathy hooked an eyebrow and looked at her sister and Steven. "Are you calling me fat?"

Steven turned away quickly and disappeared into the kitchen.

Samantha rolled her eyes. Kathy ran every morning, unless she was doing kickboxing or some other physical exercise. Fat was the last word anyone would use to describe her and even Kathy knew it.

"I just want you to be careful," Samantha said. "You and I both know all of the weirdos that are out and about."

"Okay, *Mom*." Kathy finished applying her lipstick, closed the tube, and slipped it back in her clutch.

"Who are you going with again?" Samantha asked.

Trisha.

"Is that who you've been going out with the last few weeks?" Samantha asked.

Kathy looked up at her sister. "I didn't give you a name yet."

Samantha looked confused. "You didn't? I thought I heard—"

"You must be hearing things," Kathy said. "I'm going with Trisha."

"That's what I thought you said!"

Kathy gave her sister a confused look. "*Anyway*, like I *did* say, don't wait up for me."

"Are you taking my car?"

"No, I called a cab," Kathy said. "It should be here any minute."

Samantha nodded and continued to set the table, laying out the candles and the plate settings. Ever since Kathy and Jeremy had broken up, she'd been going out to a bar or a club—or both—every weekend with Trisha. As much as Samantha liked her sister doing what she wanted without the worry of Jeremy to control her, she was concerned her sister was having a bit *too much* fun.

Kathy's heels clonked on the hardwood as she walked over to the table. "Fancy dinner?"

"Kind of an important one," Samantha murmured. "Tonight's the night."

The younger sister raised her eyebrows. "Are you ready?"

"As ready and I'll ever be."

"Do you want me to stay home?"

As much as Samantha liked the idea of Kathy actually having a night in—and a Thursday night at that, something Kathy referred to as "Thirsty Thursday"—Samantha knew she couldn't control her sister. And it would be better if she wasn't home.

"No, you go and have fun," Samantha said.

From the street, a car honked twice.

"That must be my cab," Kathy said. "Are you sure you'll be okay?"

"I'll be fine. Now go."

"Good luck," she called as she walked to the door.

Samantha yelled to her sister, "Be careful!"

As she finished setting the table, Steven came in with their food, steaming from just coming off the stove.

"That smells delicious," she said.

"Well, you did most of the work." He set the dishes on the table. "So pat yourself on the back."

"Ugh, you know my arm gets tired from doing that all the time." She smirked and allowed him to pull out her chair for her.

"Did your sister leave?" He came around the opposite side of the table and took his own seat.

"Yeah."

Good, she heard in his voice, but she didn't see his lips move so she didn't say anything.

"She's been out a lot lately," he said. "Not that I'm complaining. It gives us more time together." He reached across the table and squeezed her hand before dishing out their plates.

"She has," Samantha admitted. "I think it's still an after-effect of her breakup with Jeremy. Her way of coping with it."

Jeremy and Kathy didn't have a great relationship, she heard in Steven's voice. "Who is she even going out with?" he asked out loud.

She stared at him, confused at what was going on, but snapped out of it. This was probably just nerves about what she needed to tell him. What she tried to tell him several times but had been cut off or distracted. Tonight, she wasn't going to put up with anymore excuses.

Of course, she had said that before, too.

"Uh, Trisha," Samantha said.

Who the hell is Trisha?

"She was in Kathy's grade in high school," Samantha responded. "They were friends, not close, but they knew each other. Fell out of touch after high school and reconnected at a club."

Probably not the best influence for Kathy. "Gotcha," he said. "So an old friend?"

She narrowed her eyes, but relaxed her face when he finished dishing out their plates. "Yeah."

"Well, not to shift the subject off of your sister," he started, "but I've been doing some number crunching."

An image of a ranch-style house with a flower garden out front and a manicured lawn popped into Samantha's head. *He wants to buy a house,* she thought.

"I added up my income with yours and calculated how much the two of us would qualify for a mortgage," he said.

"Steven, we're not even married yet," she said.

"So? We can buy the house anytime and have it ready for when we are married." *Maybe move in ahead of time and get away from your sister.*

"I'm not ready to move yet," she said. "I like it here. And we haven't even set a date for the wedding yet."

"I thought we were looking at January?"

"Yeah, but we still have to decide where we're doing it, settle on a guest list, figure out what we're going to feed people, and, oh yeah, pick the actual date!"

"We can get to that," he said. "But having a place to live is important too." *Typical girl, only thinking about the wedding.*

Samantha raised her hands to her forehead. "You know what? I can't talk about this right now."

You never want to talk about this. Steven looked down at his meal and stabbed it with his fork with more force than he needed. *We're going to be living with Kathy for the rest of our lives. Sexless marriage, here we come!*

"I have something else to tell you," she said.

A baby?

"No, it's not a baby," she said quickly.

"I didn't say anything about a baby," he replied.

She got a little red in the face, her heart thumping against her chest.

"Honey, your hand's shaking." He reached across the table to take one of hers in both of his. "What's going on?" *Cancer? Is she sick? Is that why she doesn't want to commit to buying a house?*

She swallowed to try to moisten her dry throat, but it didn't work. "I'm a witch."

CHAPTER 2

Tommy Wilson crossed West 5th Street, where he parked in the lot just off Peach Street, and went in the back entrance to The 814 nightclub. Named after Erie's phone number area code, it was one of the few nightclubs in the city.

It was the last place he wanted to be after a full shift with the Erie Police Department, but it's what he needed to do to support his family. And the club was the only job that allowed him the flexibility to work around his police schedule. Plus, they liked it that he was also a police officer.

Inside, the manager and two of the bartenders were hauling cases of drinks from the cooler to the bar. Once the crowd filled in, there'd be no hope of getting through easily with a case of drinks like this. Better to be fully stocked from the beginning of the night. Tommy knew. He used to be a bartender back in college.

"Jared, how's it going?" he called out.

The manager set his case on the bar and stepped over to shake Tommy's hand. "I'm hanging in there. Glad you could come in tonight."

"No problem," he said. "Need any help with anything?"

Jared turned back to the bar where the bartender was putting the drinks away. "Nah, we've got it covered. My other bartenders should be here soon." He checked his watch.

"Anything I need to be aware of tonight?" Tommy made it a habit of checking in with Jared before his shift started. Thursday nights were when the weekend crowd started to ramp up and with the summer heat still looming over the city, people were quick to jump to hostility. Especially when they'd been drinking.

"Actually, yeah. Follow me." Jared started walking off to the hallway at the back, past the bathrooms, and through the small kitchen. They stepped into the small office and Jared grabbed a printout of a black and white security camera image. The photo was grainy, but Tommy recognized the man as a regular.

"He giving you problems?"

"Yeah, this guy's bad news," Jared said. "Tuesday night and Wednesday night—our slow nights—he got a little friendly with some of the girls. Inside security told him to stop, but he didn't."

"Of course." Tommy studied the picture some more.

"At one point, he even tried to lure a girl into the bathroom, where there's obviously no camera," Jared went on. "Louie, who was working that night—last night, I think—kicked him out. Noticed afterward that the girl he was talking to was really out of it. We think he might've spiked her drink. We got her a cab and sent her home."

"Drugs, man," Tommy said.

"Lovely little things, aren't they? Anyway, Louie told this guy he wasn't welcome back and I agree completely. Haven't heard from the girl, so I don't know if she's pressing charges or anything. He's just lucky you weren't working that night or he would've been arrested."

Should've been, Tommy thought. *The police station is right across the park and this guy still tried to pull something like this.*

"You got a name for him?" Tommy asked.

"Eugene Richards, according to his ID," Jared said. "I guess his friends call him Dickie."

"Cute."

"Can't expect a lot of ingenuity out of these guys," Jared said. "Other than him, that's all I've got for you."

Tommy handed back the picture. "Hopefully it'll be a quiet night, but I'll keep an eye out for him."

"If he gives you any trouble at the door, just flag one of the inside guys down," Jared said. "I'm not messing around with drugging girls' drinks. That's not the type of club we have here."

"I can handle this guy." Tommy turned to step out of the

office with Jared in tow. "I handle much worse on a daily basis."

"I'm sure you do." Jared patted Tommy on the back. "I wouldn't want your job."

Tommy laughed. "Most people don't. I'm going to head out and start putting up the line queues before the crowd starts. They should be showing up anytime now."

"Sounds good, Tommy," Jared said. "Be careful out there."

"I always am."

CHAPTER 3

A witch?" Steven gave Samantha a suspicious look. *How much wine has she had to drink? Did I even bring any wine out? Has she been drinking in her bedroom?*

"I'm not a drunk," she said.

"I didn't say you were." He looked at her with even more concern, before his expression turned lighter, the corners of his mouth turning up in a smile. "A witch? You're really bad at jokes sometimes." Steven pulled away and returned to his food.

"This isn't a joke," she said. "Think about all of the unexplained absences I've had over the years. The canceled dates, the forced living arrangements last month."

Steven stared at her, fork raised. He didn't say a word, but she could still hear his voice: *This is insane. A witch? She does act really strange sometimes. And there have been a lot of unanswered questions. But a witch? They're not real. Are they?*

"You're serious," he finally said.

She nodded and reached over and grabbed a flower from the vase in the center of the table.

Release the strength of my power,
To speed the life of this flower.

In an instant, the petals stretched further before wilting and turning brown.

Steven jumped back in his seat. He looked at her, trying to get a better read on her by looking in her eyes. *Is she going to hex me if I don't react the way she wants? What way am I supposed to react? Is this why she didn't want to get married in a church? Is it because she worships the devil?*

"No devil worship here," she said quickly. "Kathy and I are good witches."

"I didn't say—Kathy's a witch too?"

"Well, yeah," Samantha said with the hint of a smirk. "She's my sister. Of course she is. But listen, I'm trusting you with this because I love you. You can't tell *anyone* that Kathy and I are witches. It could…it could be really bad."

Was she not going to tell me if we weren't getting married? "So you've been lying to me all this time?" Steven got to his feet.

"Not because I wanted to." Samantha jumped up too and

came around the table. She reached for him, but he pushed her away. "I had to. For your own protection. But if we're going to be husband and wife, we can't keep secrets from each other."

"I thought we made that promise to each other a long time ago?" he asked. "Remember? You told me that I knew everything there was to know about you?"

She gulped. "I did, but—"

"But were you just lying? Just telling me what I wanted to hear? Were you ever going to tell me this if I didn't propose?"

Samantha didn't have an answer for him because she didn't know if she would have. If he didn't propose, what would be the tipping point for her telling him her secret? Would it be a threat against his life? He had been targeted by supernatural forces before. What if one finally got him and the last thing he heard before he died—the last thing he *felt*—was how the woman he loved betrayed him by keeping a secret. In that sense, Steven proposing to her forced her hand and maybe even saved his life.

Tears pooled in Samantha's eyes as she considered the possibilities and consequences of what could've happened if she had continued to keep this secret all to herself.

Steven looked at her, the pain evident on his face. "I guess I can take that as a no."

"I'm so sorry," she muttered around the lump in her throat. "I should've told you sooner."

Would she have?

"I wish I did!"

Does she really love me? Does she even know what that means?

"Steven, I love you so much." She stepped to him and reached for his hand, but he pulled away.

"I need to go." His voice was emotionless, although it was evident in his cold look what he was feeling. He turned and started for the door. *Maybe there won't be a wedding after all.*

"No!" She started following him. "We don't need to cancel the wedding! Let's just think this over."

Steven turned and looked at her. "What is this? You're a witch and suddenly you can read minds?"

Stopping in her tracks, Samantha absently played with her engagement ring. *Could* she read minds? Was that what she'd been picking up on lately? All the extra voices she'd been hearing?

"I don't—"

"Well, get out of mine!" He slammed the door behind him as he left.

More by the Author

To find more books by the author, visit
DavidNethBooks.com/Books

* * *

Subscribe to his newsletter to be the first to know of new
releases and special deals!
DavidNethBooks.com/Newsletter

* * *

If you enjoyed the book, please consider leaving a review
on Goodreads or the retailer you bought it from. Reviews
help potential readers determine whether they'll enjoy a
book, so any comments on what you thought of the story
would be very helpful!

About the Author

David Neth is the author of the Coven series, the Under the Moon series, Heat series, the Fuse series, and other stories. He lives in Batavia, NY, where he dreams of a successful publishing career and opening his own bookstore.

Also writes small town romance as D. Allen.

www.DavidNethBooks.com

www.facebook.com/DavidNethBooks

www.ingramcontent.com/pod-product-compliance
Lightning Source LLC
Chambersburg PA
CBHW021319190726
48288CB00003B/883